THE SHAWNEE TOMAHAWK

THE SHAWNEE TOMAHAWK

A true story of an
American frontier boy

1 7 8 4 - 1 7 9 7

FRANCES LEIGH WILLIAMS

illustrated by

Brinton Turkle

HENRY HOLT AND COMPANY
New York

First Edition

Library of Congress Catalog Card Number: 58–6519

99419–0118

Printed in the United States of America

To the memory of
ELLEN GLASGOW
who urged me to write this story

CONTENTS

The Shawnee Tomahawk is a true story of real people told in fiction form. This book is based on the facts as related by the hero after his return from his adventures.

THE SHAWNEE TOMAHAWK

1. Frontier Danger

Jim Moore felt a funny chilly feeling go up and down his spine. He stood absolutely still and asked himself, "What noise does that colt hear that I can't catch?"

He watched carefully to see what his favorite, a sleek black two-year-old, would do. The colt stood with ears cocked, his tail twitching nervously. The thirteen-year-old boy thought to himself, "Could the colt be hearing Indians in the woods up the mountain slopes?"

The other horses, grazing near the colt, weren't standing at attention with their heads up in the air and their ears cocked. Maybe the colt was just scary the way some young animals are. But out here on the Virginia frontier in 1784, in a long narrow valley surrounded by mountains, a fellow couldn't be too careful. Of course, his father kept on saying, "We're tucked away here in Abb's Valley. We're off the beaten track for the raiding Indians. What if there are only the Poages, the Looneys and us living here? We're as safe as anyone can be that's pushed beyond the settlements."

Jim was proud of his father. Hadn't he been a captain in the Revolution and didn't he know more about horses than any man around? But he wasn't sure his pa was right about the redskins. Besides, he sort of half-way hoped the savages might come swooping down. If only they would fight fair. But then he knew they wouldn't. He couldn't forget the way, just two years before, they'd carried off Mrs. Thomas Ingles and her children over in Burke's Garden. At this very moment he could remember the miller from over on the Bluestone River pounding on the door and shouting, "Captain Moore, them Shawnee devils done dragged Mrs. Ingles away."

Jim remembered, "And I had to stay home and guard Ma and the children while Pa and the men searched for Shawnees. But I was only eleven then and I'm thirteen now and could go after them myself."

The colt had relaxed and started eating the bluegrass that grew like a thick carpet on the valley.

At last recalling his errand, Jim leaned down to put hunks of salt on the ground and called the horses. The black colt whinnied happily and galloped forward.

The boy laughed right out loud. "That's right, handsome, show off how fast you are. You and me could catch any Shawnees alive, even that chief Black Wolf, who carried off Mrs. Ingles. Why we would catch him so quick he would never even get a chance to swing his tomahawk, would he, champion?"

As the horses neared the hunks of salt, Jim stepped back. These were some of his father's hundred animals that ranged free in the frontier valley and they were scary about getting close to people.

Jim's favorite began to nuzzle the salt but a sudden noise made him jump. The boy grumbled, "Aw shucks, Ma would bong on that ole horseshoe at this very minute."

But the lad didn't stay angry long, because that clanging noise was the call to midday dinner and there never was a time when he wasn't ready to eat. He hurried from the pasture toward the family's log home. He could see John Simpson, his father's helper and horse trainer, carrying water to the cabin, and Irish John, his pa's other hand, lugging in firewood. Jim grinned, for that would be one less armful for him to tote.

And now his little sister Mary came running out to meet him, calling, "Do hurry, Ma's made a pot of Brunswick stew and cornpones and they smell so good."

Captain Moore began the meal with a blessing. He never let the children forget that, though they were a long way from a church, they had a continuing obligation to God. With the prayer over, the Moores pitched into the food with the appetites gained by a long morning of hard work. There was no talk at first, only Captain Moore declaring, "Wife, this stew is as fine as was ever made back in our old home in Botetourt County or even as your mother made in the big house in Rockbridge."

When Jim was finally stuffed almost to his ears, he burst out, "Pa, I do believe that black colt has the makings of a race horse. You should have seen him gallop when I put out the salt."

His handsome, lean-faced father laughed merrily. "So, my lad, it isn't enough for him to be a good saddle horse."

Jim said with spirit, "Your horse Liberty, that you rode fighting in the Revolution, wasn't just an everyday riding horse."

"No, he was fast enough to have raced. But we live in wilderness country, son, far from the racetrack at Williamsburg and the silver cups men win there."

"Pa, I know we're clear across the mountains and only a short piece from Kentucky, but that doesn't keep us from training him to race."

At that moment there was a sound like the rat-tat-tat of galloping hoofs. Captain Moore held up his hand for silence at the table. Yes, some rider was certainly tearing down the valley. They all shoved their stools back and Jim dashed faster than any of them for the front door.

As the rider neared, Jim could see it was his uncle, Robert Poage, the blacksmith, who had also settled in Abb's Valley.

Captain Moore shouted out, "What brings you in such an almighty hurry, Robert?"

The burly man astride the horse breathed heavily, for he was an expert at the forge but a poor rider.

"James," he blurted, "some horse traders is over to my place. They got a string of horses for me to shoe. They're in a powerful swivet to get on their way. Aim to take the critters to Lexington or Staunton to sell or on to Winchester, if need be. I wants your Jim to keep the bellows working. Kin you spare him to me?"

Jim's chest swelled with pride. Mr. Poage had asked for *him*, not one of the hired men. But maybe his father wouldn't let him go because he was supposed to hoe the vegetable patch that afternoon. The boy felt trembly and his hands were sweating because he wanted so badly to go. He just had to see those horse traders; maybe they had been out to Kentucky, maybe they had fought Indians.

He could have kissed his mother when she said, "Why, brother Robert, I'm sure we're happy to spare you Jim. The weeding can wait but those horse traders won't."

And so Jim climbed up behind his uncle and rode off, waving gaily back to his family. There was no chance to gallop, with two on the back of the one horse, so Jim was able to ask his uncle all about the traders.

Mr. Poage could talk when he felt like it, but he had a one-track mind and right now he was thinking about shoeing those horses and how to get the work done in a hurry. He grunted in reply to some of his nephew's questions and finally went so far as to answer, "Yes, two of the men done been to Kaintuck. No, they ain't fetched the nags from there, they bought 'em from the Evanses and different ones down on the Bluestone. How do I know whether they've ever run into

Dan'l Boone? Mebbe they know him, mebbe not. You can ask them yourself."

After a few more efforts to satisfy his curiosity, Jim gave up and jogged along in silence behind his uncle. He looked up and down the valley. His mother was right when she said it was a beautiful place. Golly Ned, they didn't have bluegrass like this back in Rockbridge County. He glanced at the mountains that rose on both sides of Abb's Valley. They sure did protect the place from bitter winds and storms in wintertime, and in the summertime even the mountain slopes were good for grazing. No wonder his father said so often, "This is the finest place a man could live. There's plenty of space and plenty of freedom and no meddling neighbors to stir up trouble."

The boy was thinking about this as they jogged farther and farther from his home. Sometimes he wished for boys his own age. It got sort of lonesome at times. He shook himself. These were silly ideas for a frontier boy to have.

They had ridden over two miles now and Jim could see up ahead the Poage cabin and the log shed where his uncle had his anvil and blacksmith tools.

As they rode up to the shed a thin little man with a scraggly beard yelled, "Where in tarnation you been, Poage? Musta went clear to the Ohio River fer thet helper."

The impatient man had been currying a horse and Jim couldn't help noticing how his nervous manner had made the animal twitchy and restless.

Jim found more to his liking a brawny man with huge shoulders who was sighting down a gun he was cleaning. The big fellow said in a big deep quiet voice, "Thet's enough, Crabbe. You stop pestering the blacksmith. You was the very one said pumping the bellows wasn't no fitten work for traders. He had to go after a helper, didn't he?"

Robert Poage went swiftly to work. Jim had often helped him before and admired his uncle's way with hot iron. For hours the boy pumped the bellows and fetched water for the sweating smith to drink. When the traders weren't holding a horse to be shod, they lay around the shed talking. Crabbe, the thin little man, was the biggest talker. Crabbe would match any story another man told with some experience of his back in the French and Indian Wars, when he marched through the wilderness under a young officer named George Washington.

"At that time, ain't nobody ever heard tell of Washington."

The tale went on and on and the big man couldn't stand it any longer. He drawled out, "Yeah, yeah, Crabbe, I done heard a hundred times how you strained up them mountains out beyond Fort Cumberland and how you crossed the Youghiogheny River but ain't you and me traveled that ole Braddock Trail five or six times together? Tain't as if I hadn't been to Fort Pitt."

Crabbe snorted, "But hits a trail now with settlers alongside in places. I'll still say there wasn't no fighting in the Revolution as hot as that battle we had at that little old stockade Fort Necessity, Ezra Browne."

Browne rose to the bait and replied, "You weren't to King's Mountain when we was fighting them well-armed redcoats instead of standing alongside of them like you was."

Jim liked this kind of talk. Ever since his father had come back from fighting in the Revolution, he had begged for stories of the war.

After supper that night, Jim had to help clear the table and bring in more firewood but at last he was able to stretch out in front of the fireplace. It felt good to soak up warmth, for the spring night was chilly. His arms and back ached from pumping the bellows. Jim sniffed the smell of the men's pipe smoke. He could hardly wait till he was grown and could smoke and have big experiences to tell about.

In spite of his wanting to hear all the tales, the boy fell asleep. But a sudden argument among the traders waked him. He heard the third man, a fellow named Hoskins, saying in a mad sort of voice, "Wal, confound you, Browne, I still says my rifle was as good as that new one Dan'l Boone is so proud of. Sure Dan'l is a powerful fine shot but he ain't the onliest one on the frontier. It's just his bragging, carving on them trees the way he does, 'Dan'l Boone kilt a bar hyar,' that spread that idea."

Browne said in a voice that showed he meant business, "I ain't setting here and letting no man put himself up alongside of Boone. He learned me everything I know about the wilderness."

The two men sat glowering at each other and didn't pay any attention to Crabbe who had shot back the big iron bolt on the front door and slipped outside. But Jim saw his uncle Robert Poage glance uneasily at the door. Jim knew that the Poages lived by the same rule as his father—no one goes out of the cabin after fall of dark. On the frontier a bright man doesn't take chances unless he has to.

The boy glued his eyes on that door. In not more than a minute, the nervous little Crabbe came back in. Jim thought he'd never seen such an odd look on a man's face.

Crabbe sidled over to where the blacksmith was sitting on a stool. He said in an unsure way, "Poage, you lives in this here valley. Step outside a mite." And then, almost in a whisper, he added, "Do them owls hoot and screech like that every night? Seems awful unnatural to me for such a quiet valley."

Jim knew his uncle was a trifle deaf from pounding on iron. The boy ducked out right behind the blacksmith so he could listen too.

The weird hoot of an owl came from a nearby slope of mountain. Mr. Poage said, "Sure I hear them, Crabbe. But what of it? The woods up there is full of varmints and every kind of flying critter. Why even Jim here done shot a panther up there."

The boy was pleased by his uncle boasting of him but he had a cold feeling in his stomach. This old chap might be right. The owl had suddenly stopped hooting. The other men had come out from the cabin. Crabbe said in his squeaky, tight little voice, "Sure sounded like an Injun signal to me. And two years ago I come through Burke's Garden right after them Shawnees carried off Mrs. Ingles and the rescue party was still out after them. Them savages might just be trying again."

In the light coming through the open door, Jim

could see Ezra Browne's face grow solemn. The big man said, "Can't fool with no chance taking. Best post a lookout. We'll each take a spell through the night. I'll take the first if that sets well with you all."

Everybody agreed that was the thing to do. Jim helped his uncle check his rifle and tricky double-triggered gun. Then powder and shot were set out handy to use. Just before he dozed off, the boy glanced around the cabin. It wasn't as well built as his father's. But then Jim didn't think his uncle did anything as well as his father. For one thing he was proud of the fine way his father spoke—just as if he were still giving orders as a captain in the Revolution. And he was a good teacher too, making his children speak properly and learn to read. But most of all he was proud of his father for daring to breed and raise horses and cattle in this unprotected section. Why, he already had most a hundred horses and fifty head of cattle.

Jim felt as if he'd just gone to sleep when some kind of stirring in the cabin disturbed him. He was cross. Why was anybody shaking the floor and waking him up? Then suddenly his sleepy mind remembered. He rolled out of his quilt and found most of the men already standing at the loopholes placed high up in the walls of the cabin.

The boy headed for the corner where his uncle had put the guns early in the night. When he saw Crabbe grab up the last of his uncle's guns, Jim felt a blaze of anger sweep over him. Why in tarnation wasn't Crabbe using his own rifle? Drat it, he had counted on shooting his uncle's spare gun himself. Oh, if only he had brought along his own from home, but nobody had been looking for any trouble in Abb's Valley.

There was a scratching and clawing noise on the log wall. Crabbe had lost his nervousness now. The old frontiersman was all business. He rammed the barrel of the gun right through the chinking. Jim heard him growl under his breath, "Smack into a varmint."

Jim said quickly, "It's a double-triggered gun."

But Crabbe either didn't hear or didn't know how to handle the double device. He just kept furiously snapping the steel until Jim could tell he had broken both triggers. The boy was beside himself. He knew the Indian had gotten away. Oh, if only he could have been handling the gun!

Suddenly there was no more sound of movement outside the cabin. Ezra Browne pulled his long rifle from the loophole and peered out. He whispered, "Them skunks has pulled back behind that worm fence you got around the yard, Poage."

Hoskins muttered, "Steady. Ain't nothing but a Injun trick. They'll be back."

The wait seemed like a lifetime to Jim. He didn't feel a bit scared, just tight as a drum. The men stayed at the loopholes. His aunt Margaret and the children were so terrified that Mr. Poage ordered his nephew to sit with them and gag them if necessary to keep them from screaming.

Jim watched scornfully as he saw Crabbe throw aside the gun he had broken and fumble in the pallet where he had slept and finally drag out his own gun. Jim said to his aunt Margaret, "Maybe he was some good thirty years ago in the French and Indian War but he's a mess now. Imagine a frontiersman forgetting he had his rifle beside him in bed."

The night dragged on and, to Jim's disappointment, the Indians did not charge again. He felt cheated. When daylight showed not a sign of redskins, Poage and the traders ventured out, rifles on the ready, and searched the area around the cabin.

Ezra Browne stormed at Crabbe for missing the one shot any of them had had and wound up by saying, "Them sneaking varmints has got clear away. Couldn't have been many of 'em. When they seen so many rifles poking out they didn't dast attack. We'd best go after 'em."

Poage said firmly, "Not afore we warn the Moores of Injuns being in the valley. Besides, we need Captain Moore with us. He's worth two men in a fight."

At these words the Poage children started to cry and Mrs. Poage pleaded with her husband, "Don't go and leave us, promise on the Good Book that you won't."

"Of course I don't aim to leave you unprotected," Mr. Poage said to his wife as he patted her shoulder consolingly. Then he turned and called, "Jim, you had best guide Ezra Browne over to your pa's and tell him to set you and his men to guard your home and for him to hurry back here with Browne to help us hunt out the Shawnee."

But Jim wasn't listening to his uncle. He was staring down the valley. A man on horseback was approaching at full gallop. Even at a distance he could tell it was his father. No one else rode with such ease and control as his father.

The boy started running. He would meet his father. But he was shocked when he got close enough to see Captain Moore's face—the jaw was set, his mouth was drawn tight in a thin line and his eyes were blazing with fury. He shouted out to Mr. Poage, "Murdering Indians at my place early this morning. They scalped Richards, the young fellow that was helping me. Ripped his scalp off with a tomahawk and shot him too—a bloody business. We managed to carry Richards to the cabin and tried to ease his pain but he was done for. He died a few minutes ago. I came as soon as I could to warn you."

"The heathen devils was here too but we was luckier than Richards. We was all in the cabin with the door and shutters fastened tight and on account of these men being here, we had so many guns the savages pulled back."

Jim blurted out, "Pa, how could they scalp Richards and not get anyone else? Where was he?"

"Not far from the cabin."

And now everyone was asking questions all at the same time. Captain Moore held up his hand and said in his old army voice, "Quiet. I'll tell you the details. Right at daybreak, Richards went out to put some deer skins in soak so he could dress them. As he left the cabin, I heard Irish John ask him why he was taking his rifle when he was only going a few hundred yards. Richards chuckled and said, 'Figured I might get a deer this time of day over near the salt hunks. If you hear me shoot and call out loud, some of you come running with the dogs.'

"Irish John laughed at him and said, 'Tain't likely,'

but in a few minutes I heard a rifle shot and Richards call out. I grabbed two of the dogs and ran down the ravine and up the slope toward the woods. There I found Richards writhing in agony, his head scalped and blood pouring from a bullet wound."

Mrs. Poage cried out, "Oh, brother James, this is too much to stand. Dismount and you and Robert make plans to leave Abb's Valley."

"Hush, wife, this be business fer men," Poage said, but his voice was kind as he urged his wife to go back inside the cabin.

Captain Moore was speaking again. "No time to waste. Robert, lend your horse to my boy. He and I'll go tell Abb Looney the bad news. Little as I like it, there's nought for it but we must all go now to the fort on the Bluestone till this band of Shawnees leaves our section."

Poage nodded his head up and down in solemn agreement and told Jim to fetch a horse.

Within an hour the three families from Abb's Valley and the horse traders were on their way to the fort. Once there, Jim felt a funny sort of letdown. Other settlers had come in from the nearby valleys and the small blockhouse fort was terribly crowded. Some men stood guard in the fort while others went out to scout for the Indian raiders.

Jim was considered too young to go out with the scouts and, like the others, was required to stay in the fort or immediately outside. There was no way he could avoid hearing his aunt Margaret hammering at his uncle Robert about leaving Abb's Valley. She would declare, "It's not fair to the children. They're scared plum out of their wits. They can hardly get to sleep and when they do they moan all night."

Finally Jim's father answered one of these remarks, saying, "But, sister, this has happened just once in our valley and the Shawnees may never come near our places again."

"James, you have a reputation for being fearless. If you're bound and determined to stay, that's your business. But, I'm a mother and the good Lord expects me to look out for my little ones. I'm perfectly willing for Robert to let you buy our part of the valley."

And so it was settled. Robert Poage agreed to sell his holdings in Abb's Valley to Captain Moore and to take his wife and children back to less exposed Montgomery County. They would be happier at the farm of Colonel and Mrs. David Cloyd and they'd be welcome, Poage declared, for Mrs. Cloyd was his cousin.

When the scouting parties had covered the entire surrounding area and could find no trace of the Indians, Captain Moore stated he would take his family back to Abb's Valley. Jim was pleased with his father's decision. He certainly was glad his father and mother had decided to stick it out. And the Looneys were going back too. Abb Looney was nearly as crazy about that valley as Jim's father. Well, no wonder, wasn't he supposed to be the first white man to explore it away back in 1766, and wasn't it named for him?

As they rode over the ridge and down into the valley, Jim heard his father say to his mother in a low, quiet voice, "Martha, you and I love independence and plenty of land around us that belongs to us. You're braver than most of the men and I'm proud of you. No doubt about it, freedom is worth danger."

But, in the days to come, Abb Looney was to find that his wife didn't feel the same as Mrs. Moore. She was almost sick with fear of the Shawnees swooping down again. Her nervousness was so great that Mr. Looney finally asked Captain Moore if Jim could spend his nights with them. "It would give me another gun in the house—the boy's fast on the rifle. The wife's begging me to move away and I figgered having the lad with us of nights might make her feel safe enough to stay."

2. His Own Colt

During the days Jim worked at home, and before sundown he went to the Looneys' cabin. It was decided that Jim would stay on guard to watch the cabin the first part of each night and Mr. Looney would then wake and watch until dawn.

After the family setttled down to sleep each night, the boy found it lonely sitting up. The croakings of a bull frog and the occasional snort of a deer were bad enough, but the more eerie hoot of a distant owl made him downright twitchy. He strained trying to decide whether they were real animal noises or Indian signals. He struggled to keep his eyes open all the time but sometimes he cat-napped. He had dozed off like this one night when he was jerked awake by a rustling outside. Mr. Looney was snoring so hard that Jim had trouble recognizing the sound.

Something was going on in the woods of the nearby mountain slope. Jim pressed his ear to a loophole to listen. His whole body tightened up like a drawn bow. He noticed his hands were clammy with sweat as he changed his grip on his rifle. He knew he ought to wake Mr. Looney but he wanted to handle the danger by himself. Besides there was no use stirring up poor Mrs. Looney and the children if it wasn't Indians, Jim reasoned.

Now he could make out that the noise was the whir of birds disturbed from their night perch on a tree limb. The birds flew over the cabin as if seeking refuge in the valley. This was strange for nighttime. What had scared them? The air was filled with the hideous noise of a screech owl. Jim could feel the hair rising on his neck and his mouth was as dry as an old bone. Were Indians creeping through those woods? He wet his lips and jutted his chin out to steady himself. If he waked the family, the children would start crying and he would no longer be able to hear what was happening outside. No, he'd not wake them, better to take the chance alone.

Anxiously he peered through the small round opening. If only there were a moon. But then, he knew, Indians wouldn't expose themselves on a bright night. There were some stars out but clouds kept covering them. Once the clouds blew over and Jim thought he saw a tall weed waving in the night air. What was making it move? he worried. All the time he kept his eye on a tree that stood at a distance, beyond the house yard. Jim knew that Mr. Looney had left the tree standing to give shade by day to his milk cows. But the boy muttered over the stupidity of having left it there, for it cast a huge black shadow. To himself he said, "Plenty easy for an Indian to hide in its boughs and make a fast run for the cabin. Wouldn't even have to do that. He could shoot flaming arrows from there right up on the roof and set fire to the cabin."

Jim turned cold and gasped. He was sure now something was moving the bough of that tree. He clutched his rifle even more fiercely. He thought it looked like someone crawling out on the limb. At that instant, the body dropped to the ground and started toward the cabin. Jim took one fast look down his sights and fired. He was shaking for fear he might have missed.

Instantly every member of the Looney family was awake. Abb Looney was roaring, "Is it Injuns, boy, is it?"

Jim could not answer. He was too busy loading his gun again.

Mr. Looney peered out the hole, muttering, "Can't see nothing."

"Over there just inside the yard. I hit him. Can't you see the body heaving?"

Mrs. Looney was sobbing and wailing, "Oh I knew they'd come back after us. I know it's the Injuns. Oh, see if it's a red savage. Abb, you've got to find out, we just have to know."

"Ain't no sensible man going to risk that. I ain't

budging out of this cabin and get shot at if it be murdering Shawnee varmints."

But Jim wasn't feeling sensible. He was bursting with impatience to know if he really had shot a redskin. Quick as a flash of lightning, he pushed back the bolt of the door and ran swiftly towards the fallen form at the end of the yard. Whether Indian or animal he could not tell, at first, due to the distance. Suddenly the body gave a writhing shudder and then was still. Jim had his gun cocked and ready. His heart was pounding like a cannonade.

He jerked up short. In front of him, stretched on the grass, was a wildcat, the biggest bobtail he had ever seen. He waited to make sure the vicious woods' animal was dead before he moved forward and kneeled down by it. Yes, there was the wound and the blood from it.

The boy raced back to the cabin with the good news that it was an animal and not an Indian. But the strain had been too much for Mrs. Looney. Her eyes were wild and she announced in a violent tone, "Never, never will I spend another night in this God-forsaken place nor will I let my children. Absalom Looney, you're moving us out of here, say you are, just say it."

The distraught woman choked on the last words in a burst of sobs. Abb Looney had to promise to move away before he could stop her anguish.

At the first streak of dawn, Jim was sent to his home to tell the family that the Looneys were leaving. Mrs. Moore started cooking food for the travelers to take on their journey to a safer home. Jim and his father went to the Looneys' to help load their belongings on their stoutest wagon. All the Moores came to say good-by and Irish John and John Simpson helped Mr. Looney get the cattle herded up and started down the valley. Mrs. Looney drove the wagon with the children and belongings and Abb Looney, leading a second horse, rode herd on the cattle.

Captain and Mrs. Moore were cheerful as they called good-by and the children tried to be cheerful too. But soon the small ones were crying. It was a sad sight to see the last of their neighbors leaving. Jim found he had a lump in his throat. He knew it was going to be lonely without any other family in Abb's Valley. But he wasn't crying. He had killed that wildcat and he would just kill any Indian that might show up the same way.

In the weeks ahead, the heavy work of planting the crops kept the Moores busy. But on Jim's fourteenth birthday he received a big surprise. His father led him out to the pasture and pointing to Jim's favorite, the black colt, said, "Son, he's all yours and I want you to learn to train him yourself. I think the colt has special promise."

"You give him to me for my very own and I can name him?"

"Exactly what I mean. And don't forget that he's a son of Yorick, the finest Arabian I've ever owned or ever hope to."

"He's going to be the finest of all Yorick's colts. Pa, I'm going to call him Prince Charlie. See that patch of white hair that looks like a crown up on his forehead. Ever notice it?"

Captain Moore chuckled, "No, lad. I'm more inter-

ested in hard, clean limbs on an animal and your Prince
Charlie has them. What's to be your first step with him?"

"Well, the colt's been running with the others so
long he's shy of a human. I aim to make friends first,
give him scraps of sugar loaf and a carrot now and
then. I'll pat him and soon he'll be letting me run my
hands over his back and neck. Then I'll get a halter
on him."

"That's the way I want you to start. Just remember
what a wonderful memory a horse has. Never run after
him and scare him or he'll hold it against you all his
life."

The summer weeks passed slowly. Each day was
packed with work but whenever Jim could snatch a
minute, he spent it with Prince Charlie. He was now
teaching the young horse to follow the leading rein.
The boy talked quietly to him and patted him each
time before he attached the ten-foot rein to the halter.
Jim would start off at a walk and the Prince walked
quietly behind. Then the boy would jog along faster
and this pleased the two-year-old colt much more.

The Prince, however, did not like to pass old stumps
or fallen logs or even a pile of stones.

Captain Moore said, "You'd better walk him right
up to them for a few days."

Jim did this and after he had led the Prince straight
up to a clothes line where garments fluttered in the
wind and the colt did not shy, Jim could brag that the
Prince had gotten over being scared. He said to Mr.
Simpson, "Must be about time for a bit in his mouth."

The bow-legged horse trainer exploded, "Nowhere

near time. But you can start him now on the twenty-foot rein."

Jim would stand in one place and pivot around as Prince Charlie moved in a great circle. The boy loved to roll out the commands, "Wa-a-a-alk, tr-r-rot, ha-a-alt!" just the way he had heard Mr. Simpson do it.

In August the trainer finally let him put a bit in the colt's mouth. They tied Prince Charlie in the stable and then Mr. Simpson handed Jim a mouthing bit, murmuring, "Now slip it in easy, James, and make sure the beads of it just touch his front teeth. Be you sure he can't take the beads in his teeth? Well, let him play with the bit and get used to it."

Two weeks later Prince Charlie was ready for the snaffle bit, but Jim was getting awfully tired of training him on that long rein.

One late August morning Captain Moore asked at breakfast, "Why don't you lay an old saddle out now for your horse to get used to? Walk him over it. Rub it against his neck and shoulders. In two or three days you can lay it quietly on his back. Just don't let it fall and frighten him."

Soon Jim was reaching up and pressing hard on the saddle to get the Prince used to weight. Oh, how he itched to climb up on the Prince's back and gallop down the field! Sometimes he would dream of rescuing someone from Shawnee Indians and other days he'd dream of riding the Prince in some famous race. But every day he hounded Simpson with the question, "When can I mount?"

The shrewd little Englishman replied, "Now, lad-

die, ye're so sure yon colt's to be a racer, we'd best bide
our time a wee snip. Wait till the captain gives the
order."

But Jim felt he'd waited long enough. He was sure
the time had come. So one night when his mother had
set before them a fine supper and his father was in
grand good humor, Jim put the question to him directly. "Pa, can't I mount and ride Prince Charlie tomorrow? Please. It's the fifth of September and you
said I could in September."

"Maybe so, lad, if we finish cutting and shocking the
corn. We've got to get ahead of that rain that's about
due. You'll be hankering after corn for your colt when
the winter cold sets in. I'm pleased with how much
you've learned from Simpson. You know he worked
with race horses back in England. I'm glad he stayed
on to work with me even after he'd finished his term
as an indentured servant and earned his freedom. Why
Yorick, the Arabian, won't let anyone else handle him.
So I know your colt and you are both ready, because
Simpson told me you were."

When Jim awoke the next morning, he bounced
straight out of bed. This was going to be about the
most exciting day of his life. At last he was going to
mount Prince Charlie and actually ride him. He
wouldn't go far this first time, of course, but still he'd
be riding his very own horse. He whistled a gay tune
and tore down from the loft where he slept alongside
of Irish John and Mr. Simpson.

Jim ran over to his mother, who was stirring the
coals from last night's fire. Impulsively he gave her a
kiss on her forehead. Mrs. Moore looked pleased and

commented, "Many a day since you've done that, son. It pleasures me to see you so extra happy and gay."

The boy raced out of the cabin door to get his chores done as fast as possible. First he brought in great arm-fuls of wood and built up the fire, announcing, "Cook piles of victuals, Ma, I'm hungry as a bear."

"And when weren't you, young man? You eat more than Irish John and that's really saying something. But I'm glad we always have plenty to fill your hollow legs." Mrs. Moore smiled as she said it.

Jim picked up two empty pails and headed for the spring. On his return he crouched on the hearth and filled the heavy iron kettle that hung on a hook in the fireplace.

Soon breakfast was ready and Jim did full justice to the hot porridge served with cream, the corn meal cakes which his mother cooked on the iron spider in the fireplace, frizzing them till they had brown lace edges, and thick home-cured strips of bacon. The boy washed it all down with a big mug of milk.

As his father had predicted, it was a busy day. Jim did the same work as his father, Mr. Simpson and Irish John, swinging a big corn knife. There was rhythm to it and the strong lad liked it. The ripple of muscles under his shirt made him feel good. However, his thoughts were all of his colt, and of having his first ride.

Captain Moore, working next to his son, sensed the boy's worry that they'd never finish the corn. He called, "Don't fret, Jim, if we keep plugging away, I reckon we'll shock the last stalks by four-thirty. Then you and Simpson can sashay right out to the meadow and get hold of Prince Charlie for the saddling."

His father's estimate wasn't far wrong. At twenty minutes before five, by Captain Moore's great thick gold watch, the men cut the last brittle corn stalk and stacked it in a shock shaped like an Indian tepee.

John Simpson, whistling through a gap in his teeth, came toward Jim and shouted, "Glad enough I am that that's done. Now, lad, let's get to some interesting work."

Suddenly Jim wasn't tired any more.

"James, we'll lead Prince Charlie off by himself down near the stable shed. I'll walk him a bit whilst you fetch the saddle."

Jim stood looking at his colt, who was nuzzling him affectionately.

"Mr. Simpson, doesn't that white spot on his forehead look like a crown to you?"

"Ah, laddie, it just might at that. Can't say as how I ever saw a crown back in the old country though His Majesty George III cert'nly had one handy."

The boy persisted, "But you saw those signs on the coaching inns you told me about, the Royal George and the others. They must have had pictures of kings with crowns on them, didn't they?"

The trainer gave his cackling laugh. "If ye're bent on making him royal-like, we'd best be at teaching him a thing or two."

Jim was so eager to see what would happen when he put his weight on the colt's back that he was all thumbs hoisting the saddle in place. The Prince stood patiently while Jim tightened the girth band, for he was used to this by now.

However, when Mr. Simpson went forward and held

his head, the young horse rolled his eyes back to see what was going on. Jim quickly put his foot in the stirrup and lay across the saddle. Prince Charlie shook his body but moved forward when led by Mr. Simpson. His owner continued to lie loosely across the saddle.

The English trainer said, "Ha-a-alt."

Jim dismounted and patted his horse. Then they repeated the performance three more times. Finally Simpson said, "Now put your leg over quietly."

And this time Jim mounted, swung his leg over quietly and sat in the saddle. The trainer released Prince Charlie's head and Jim rode forward. He felt like the king of the universe.

The ride was a short one to prevent injury to the Prince's tender back muscles.

"Now, James, here be your sister Mary with a scrap of sugar loaf. Give it to your mount for it has been a trying experience for the young Prince." Stroking the horse, he clucked, "There's no royal road to learning, you know, even with your crown setting up there, Prince Charlie, and besides don't be forgetting this be a republic we live in."

No horse in all Virginia received a more loving rubdown than Prince Charlie did that afternoon from his proud master.

At the supper table everyone talked about the colt.

"I'd like to have seen you do that, son," Mrs. Moore told Jim when she had a chance to speak, "but baking day's one time when I can't wander far from the house. Here, Jim, have another slice of my hot bread."

She turned to her husband. "We're getting mighty

low on corn meal, Captain. Are you planning to go to the mill soon?"

Captain Moore looked thoughtful and the children waited for his reply because these trips were special events in the quiet life at Abb's Valley. At the mill, a good twelve miles away, news of the outside world and of the other settlers in the mountains could be picked up. And sometimes their father brought back presents when he met up with a trader at the mill.

Finally the weather-tanned man with the keen eyes spoke. "I thought to put the trip off a week or two longer but I reckon 'tis best not to if you're running low on meal. Do you have much wheat flour on hand, wife?"

"No, Captain, the merest half a poke."

"Then Simpson had best ride over tomorrow and take both corn and wheat to be milled."

Jim's heart sank. That meant they couldn't give Prince Charlie his next training.

Captain Moore noticed the gloom on his son's face. "What ails you, James?" he demanded. "Did you eat too heavy after a hard day in the field?"

"Oh no, sir. Ma's cooking always sets well with me."

"Then what is it? Speak up. I'll have no sulks."

Jim hung his head a second. He seemed always to be after his father for something these days. Then he managed to answer, " 'Tis just, sir, that I so much wanted to train Prince Charlie again with Mr. Simpson."

"Since you've mounted him once, you must repeat tomorrow. I had clean forgotten that. I'll go myself to the mill. The faster we get him used to your weight, the sooner you can really ride Prince Charlie."

"This be no steeplechase," Mr. Simpson protested mildly. He hated to lose out on going to the mill, for he liked to see people and leave the work routine behind every now and then. He glanced at Captain Moore, hoping he'd include him in the trip. But the captain had finished with the subject and had picked up the big family Bible.

"Young Miss Mary, you and your sister Jane hop over here close to me," he said as he opened the Bible and motioned for quiet. "First let us give thanks for that fine yield of corn. It will provide well this winter."

Then in his deep voice, the head of the household read the Nineteenth Psalm slowly and clearly so that the young people could understand. It was one of Jim's favorites and he knew it practically by heart. But tonight his thoughts strayed from the rhythm of the words. The boy was reliving the afternoon's events. The noise of his father closing the book snapped him out of his daydream. Stools and benches were pushed back and Mrs. Moore and the girls started clearing the table. Irish John sidled over to pick up his cornet and piped softly on it as he and Simpson went to the barn to finish the night chores. The captain sat on at the table, drawing up a list of things to take to the mill and items he needed to obtain there next day.

It was his little brother Joe's turn tonight to help with the dishes so Jim was free. There was a thrilling adventure book he was reading all about Valentine and Orson and wild animals. He reached for it and stretched out in front of the fire. But he was not to read long. When Simpson came back in he pulled a stool up to the table and started talking about horses with Captain Moore. Jim was anxious to find out what was going to happen next in the book but he couldn't go on when he heard Simpson say, "Captain, James has the natural touch with horses and he's teachable. He did well today with Prince Charlie and you know, Captain Moore, that colt shows promise."

Jim listened for his father's reply and was bowled over to hear him say, "Yes, the two-year-old reminds me more of my horse Liberty that I rode in the Revolution than any four-legged thing I've owned since."

Little Mary and Joe both heard their father speak of Liberty and ran over to him. The pretty seven-year-old girl looked up at her father and begged, "Oh, Papa dear, please tell us a story. It's been so long since you have. But please tell us one about Liberty and not about Indians."

Jim saw his mother glance up to see if the solid shutters were closed and barred over the loophole windows.

But Captain Moore was put out by his child mentioning Indians. He said rather severely, "Odds are strong, young miss, that the savages will never come back. Those were just straggling scouts and Poage and the horse traders gave them a bad scare. Besides I don't like any young one of mine to speak of being afraid."

Mrs. Moore quickly added in a serene voice, "Why, of course we're safe in our lovely grassy valley when we have such fine shots here as your father, Mr. Simpson and Irish John."

Jim loved his mother for saying brave things like

that, for he knew she never forgot the possibility of danger here on the frontier.

Irish John spoke up now from the corner where he was mending a shoe. "Nivver fergit Master Jeemie and the way he kin handle a rifle. That were a powerful fine shot he made at that wildcat at Looney's."

Captain Moore frowned. He must get the talk away from danger to Abb's Valley or the children would never sleep a wink that night. He asked, "How'd you like me to tell about when I moved the family down here in the fall of 1775 and how we camped out at night?"

Little Mary said, "Oh no, Papa, we've heard about that often from Mama. You tell us about when you lived back in Rockbridge and used to ride into Lexington to the shops and go to the Presbyterian Church every Sunday."

Joe broke in scornfully, "Naw, that's what girls like to hear. Come on, Pa, and tell us about Liberty and fighting in the Revolution."

3. Captured!

Captain Moore cleared his throat with a loud harrumph and began, "You children have heard me say that when we were fighting for independence, our company of riflemen were all mounted. When we set out from Bluestone River, we took our own horses with us. I rode my fast black named Liberty. He was a handsome animal and knew what I was thinking before I did. We'd been through a lot of campaigns together when this happened along toward the end of the Revolution."

Jim chuckled softly, "It's going to be the story about that time at the battle of Guilford Court House down in North Carolina."

And so it proved. Jim, sprawled out in front of the fire, felt as if he were taking part in the battle against the British. His father could make words march along and say something. He wasn't like some of the silent men down on the Bluestone, nor did he speak roughly like Robert Poage. Well, he'd had an education and he loved to read. At that moment Jim was even glad that his father tried to make him speak good clear English. He listened attentively now to the tale.

"The battle was raging over a goodly area. The noise was very great. The Britishers had a way of hauling up six-pound cannon and bam, bam, bamming with them. There was rifle firing and horses whinnying with fear or pain and officers shouting out their orders.

"All that mounts up to a mighty din and it had made our horses nervous. Liberty was a high-spirited animal and still young. When I had tied him up earlier, so that our company could take the first charge of the day on foot, I had passed the reins over the end of a tree limb. I had made a noose so Liberty could move around while I was gone."

Joe said in his high voice, "Whew, I bet Liberty was prancing from all that noise. I know Yorick would have been."

"Yes, he was badly frightened and sidestepping around in a circle. I couldn't get him to stand still so I could untie the noose I had made out of the reins. Then I heard the British dragoons charging toward us and one of my men yelled, 'Cut the reins, Captain, or they'll capture you for sure. Cut 'em' "

Little Mary cried excitedly, "And did you, Pa?"

"Certainly not. I shouted back, 'No, I won't,' because once I had cut those reins, I couldn't have ridden Liberty back into the fight against the dragoons. So I used every ounce of strength in my body and made a tremendous leap up in the air and someway managed to grab that limb and wrench it from the tree. Providence must have helped me."

Jim said, "But that still didn't rip the reins loose from the limb."

"No, but I just sprang up in the saddle and rode off with the limb dangling. Liberty was frantic and took the bit in his mouth and started galloping directly *toward* the enemy.

"Well, for me it was then or never. I had to forget the Redcoats and somehow do something about those reins. At last I got them loose, regained control and poor Liberty almost thanked me when I took over again. By that time, however, we were within a few yards of the British. I thought we were gone but I managed to wheel Liberty around and the black responded nobly."

Mary clapped her hands in delight.

The captain smiled and continued, " 'Twas a mad, mad ride back to my own ranks. If Liberty and I had been on a race course, I think we would have broken all kinds of records. 'Twas our speed that saved us from the bullets whizzing around us. You should have heard the roars of delight from my men as Liberty and I regained the ranks. Almost instantly we charged against the enemy. So you see why I valued Liberty so highly. He made that crazy dash but he also saved my life."

Jim said excitedly, "You watch Prince Charlie, he's going to be just like him."

Mary climbed up on her father's lap and patted his cheek, murmuring, "You were so brave."

The captain laughed gently. "I don't know who was more afraid, Liberty or myself, but we pulled through. Most soldiers will tell you, boys, that they've been scared. The big thing is not to give up."

Reaching for his pipe, the captain said, "Off to bed now, young ones. I don't want to see any sleepyheads in the morning."

Because of his fourteen years, Jim was not in the early-bed crowd. He threw more logs on the glowing fire and once more stretched out on the floor to read by the light of the dancing flames. Almost immediately he was lost in the perilous adventures of Valentine and Orson. The hissing of the fire added an eerie note to the wild tale.

He barely looked up when his father said, "It's getting late, son."

But Captain Moore came over to tap his pipe out and place it on the mantel and said, "I've been sitting there dreaming, Jim, of the day when I can buy all this valley and we'll raise so many horses we'll be selling them into Kentucky as fast as that country really opens up. You'd best turn in, lad, we have a heavy day tomorrow."

"Let me just finish the chapter Pa, I'm in such an exciting part."

"You may finish this one. Then go to bed, son."

Jim read on in great gulps, unable to stop. He just had to find out how the scary tale would end. It was very late when he at last banked the fire with ashes. Sleepily he climbed up the ladder to the loft and stretched out on his pallet. But even though he was tired, he couldn't get to sleep right away. John Simpson's deep breathing made a whistling noise and Irish John snored loudly, but Jim felt suddenly lonely. He had the unhappy feeling of being afraid. He shook it off and fell asleep. In fact he slept so soundly that he could hardly get up in the morning.

Right after breakfast Captain Moore told Jim, "I want you to chop wood as usual for the cooking and then go over to the field by the cabin the Poages lived in, where I've been grazing the big group of horses. Trusty's there in that batch and I want you to catch him and fetch him back for me to ride to the mill. I aim to eat about noon and then head out, so don't dawdle around bringing Trusty back."

It was rarely that Mrs. Moore ever questioned her husband's orders, but she hesitantly asked now, "Don't you think that's a far piece for the boy to go alone?"

" 'Tis broad daylight, my dear wife, and peaceful as can be. Of course I wouldn't send him after dark but I certainly can now. He's near a man in size."

The boy was very puffed up over his father's likening him to a man.

Now young Joe started begging to go along. But Mrs. Moore said, "No, Joseph, you had best stay with me. I want you to keep the fire going under the pot of water. I've a heavy wash to do. And you keep the dogs from running after Jim so they won't scare the horses when he's trying to catch Trusty."

By the time Jim was ready to leave, the morning sun was hot. The boy picked up his battered old shade hat and jammed it on his head. He opened his coarse cotton shirt at the neck, yanked up his tough work pants and yelled at Joe, "Hang on to the dogs till I'm out of sight."

He started gaily up the valley, whistling that tune that Irish John was always playing. The thick grass felt good under his bare feet. He was glad it was a long time until snowfall, when he would have to put on shoes. They lived too far from a cobbler's shop to wear out shoe leather when it wasn't necessary.

He got to wondering what had made his mother seem fearful about him. It certainly wasn't like her. Somebody had usually ridden with him over to the Looneys' when he was sleeping there. But that was back during the Indian scare. He glanced up at the mountains that surrounded the valley. The ridge looked every bit of the 3400 feet it was supposed to be. A cloud blotted out the sun for a moment, and suddenly the mountains seemed dark and menacing. For the first time in his life Jim felt small, alone, really almost deserted. He shook himself to get rid of the unpleasant feeling. Even in the Looney cabin that night, shooting at the wildcat, he hadn't felt like this. Bits from the book he had read the night before came rushing into his mind and he became convinced that a wild beast was going to pounce and tear him to shreds. He was clammy from the feeling of an unknown danger, of something he could neither see nor hear.

He longed to turn around and go home. He gritted his teeth and forced himself to keep moving forward. Hadn't his father said only last night that any honest man knew what it was to be afraid but must never give in to it?

And so the boy trudged grimly on. When he had gone nearly two miles he could see the deserted Poage cabin. The empty house was a lonely sight, so different from the time when his uncle and aunt had lived there. Jim wondered if a panther could possibly have prowled down from the woods and made his lair in the cabin. His heart was beating fast and his hands were wet with perspiration. Why was he so worked up? It made him angry but he could not get rid of that feeling of something terrible about to happen.

Jim was nearing the field where Trusty and the other horses were pastured. His father's riding horse was standing motionless with head up. Jim put his fingers to his lips to give his usual whistle but his hand was shaking. He felt ashamed of the trembling. Why, he was acting like an old woman, he told himself. Repeatedly he turned to look behind, expecting to see some wild animal like the ones in his Orson and Valentine book. Finally he managed a whistle and Trusty started toward him at a gallop. The boy's spirits rose. In a couple of minutes he'd be up on Trusty's back and riding for home. He waited, eager to plunge his hands into Trusty's mane and leap on his back.

"Here boy," he called, but the words turned into a scream as he felt himself seized from behind, his head held in a vise from which he could not shake himself free. He screamed again with all his might. This was no animal. It must be an Indian.

He was right. A guttural voice spoke harshly, *"Chit, che, chack."*

Now his shoulder was gripped and he was roughly turned around to face a massive Indian with a savage face. Terrified, but holding his head bravely erect, Jim took a good long look at his captor. The man was about six feet tall and magnificently built with heavily muscled chest and arms. The boy was astonished to see that the Indian had a black beard. Why, redskins weren't supposed to have beards. Wait a minute though, hadn't they said that the Shawnee chief who led the raid on Burke's Garden and carried off Mrs. Ingles had a beard? He stared more closely at the savage. Yes, half the hair on his head was shaved off and there was a crooked scar running down to his eyebrow. That was just the description John Simpson had given him of Black Wolf after the Ingles raid.

Silently two young braves appeared and stood behind Black Wolf. One of them did not look over eighteen and kept prancing around swinging his tomahawk. A sharp command from the black-bearded chief stopped the whirling.

Black Wolf put his hand on Jim's back and pushed him forward. With his tomahawk the Indian pointed to the horses grazing just beyond the Poage cabin. Trusty was back with the other horses but he was not grazing. The animal stood on the alert, watching the approach of the men. As they got near to the horses, Black Wolf opened a buckskin pouch hanging at his waist and drew out salt. He held it out to Jim. The

stuff had a reddish color and the boy guessed the Indians
had gotten it at the salt lick west of Abb's Valley.

Jim decided his best course was to play dumb. He
just stood with his bare feet planted wide apart in
the bluegrass and looked down at the salt as if he didn't
know what to do with it.

Black Wolf leaned close and pointed menacingly
with his tomahawk first at the salt, then to the horses,
growling, "*Nepepimma, nepepimma.*" When Jim continued to look stupid, the red man with difficulty muttered something that sounded like "Ketchee hoss" and
raised his tomahawk right over Jim's head. His expression was wild and threatening.

Jim Moore had no choice. He moved toward the
horses, a young brave keeping right at his side. He held
the salt in an outstretched hand and spoke softly to
Trusty. His mind began to work again. If he could
mount Trusty and ride a wild zig-zag course around
the field scattering the other horses as he went, maybe
he could escape from the fire of Black Wolf's gun.

But the young Indian knew that any captive would
attempt escape, and the minute Jim seized Trusty's
mane, the redskin tried to leap on before the boy could.
This terrified Trusty, who went charging away at a
hard run. None of the Moore horses was easy to mount
or handle, for they were ridden so little. Jim knew he
had to act in a very quiet way if he was to calm Trusty
and escape. Now the young brave flourished his tomahawk again and signaled the boy toward Trusty, hissing
the word "*meshewa,*" which Jim knew must mean
horse.

Jim realized that the Indians had no idea of ever letting him get on Trusty's back. They would never give him such a chance to escape. But they persisted in trying to make him capture the riding horse. The frontier boy decided his only chance was to stall for time. Maybe, just maybe, his father would be in such a hurry to go to the mill that he would come after Trusty himself. He pretended now that he was trying to catch the sorrel. He made one approach after another but in such a nervous way that Trusty became more and more excited. All the other horses had long ago galloped away and now his father's saddle horse whinnied wildly and headed off.

Black Wolf barked an order. Instantly the young brave pushed Jim toward the chief. The bearded man poked his tomahawk in the boy'a ribs and forced him to turn around. They started single file in the direction of Ridge Mountain. The young Indians were muttering fiercely. Over and over Jim heard the word *meshewa,* so he knew they were raging over not capturing one of his father's handsome horses. But Black Wolf now growled one word, in a warning tone, "*Kesathwa.*"

Jim saw the braves jerk their eyes upward at the sun. It was getting high in the heavens. They broke into a fast dogtrot, leading the way, with Jim next, and massive Black Wolf guarding the rear.

When the Indians reached the edge of the grassy valley, they halted at a big thicket of haw bushes and pulled out blankets and cooking kettles which they had hidden there. Black Wolf searched Jim to make sure he had no knife under the coarse shirt he wore. The boy hated the touch of the savage's prying fingers, the strong odor of the man.

The Shawnees quickly strapped on their belongings and headed up the ridge. They moved at a fast pace even though the mountainside provided rough going. Jim observed every inch of the way they were taking. This area was very familiar to the boy. He had hunted all over it. He kept brushing against bushes to try to leave a mark and broke twigs as often as he dared. If he could only keep this up, his father could easily locate their trail.

But Black Wolf noticed what his captive was doing and angrily shook his tomahawk over the lad's head. He pointed in an accusing way to the broken twigs and growled, "No-o." He pronounced the word as if it had two syllables but Jim realized that this brutal raider had picked up a few English words from his previous victims. Now the bearded man swung the tomahawk right by Jim's eyes, making it clear that he would kill the boy if he continued marking the trail.

For a while Jim went along quietly, trying to put Black Wolf off guard. Then he said to himself, "Got to leave some signs for Pa to find or they'll never know which way we've gone. This ground's so rocky that no footprint shows."

Thinking that his captor was no longer watching him, the boy watched for little patches of soil on the trail and dug his big toe in to scratch a mark. It did not take Black Wolf long to see what was going on. He howled out a long list of terrible-sounding Indian words and stood stock still before the boy, ready to

crash the tomahawk down and split his head. The
young braves handed their chief some leather thongs,
urging him to bind the boy's hands and keep him prisoner rather than kill him. Black Wolf stood thinking
it over, then suddenly pushed the braves away and,
seizing Jim roughly, pushed his head down to the
earth to force him to look at the marks he had just
made. Once again he shouted "No-o" and shook his
tomahawk in one hand and his rifle in the other. Jim
knew he would be killed instantly unless he agreed.
Reluctantly he nodded his head up and down, agreeing
to Black Wolf's order.

A gloom sank over the boy as he realized that it
would be extremely difficult for any search party to
pick up their trail. He wondered if by now they had
become alarmed back home and started the hunt for
him. He couldn't help remembering how useless their
hunt had been for the Indians the morning after the
savages had attempted to attack the Poages.

The going was rough due to the thorny greenbrier
and the great forest giants fallen across their way. These
old trees were covered with moss and were not easy
to climb over. Meanest of all, though, were the tangles
of vines they sometimes had to fight. They were traveling uphill part of the time and down rocky banks
at other times. Jim's bare feet were tough, but they
were used to the grassy valley and felt the rocks.

The discomfort of his feet gave the boy a burning
wish for his heavy boots, which were on a shelf over
his pallet back home. The longing to protect his feet
almost drove other thoughts out of his mind. Once or
twice he recalled with pleasure that the Indians hadn't

been able to capture Trusty and that his colt Prince Charlie was safe in the valley. These Indians had evidently been on a scouting raid or there would be more of them. Maybe they'd soon join up with the rest of the party.

But mostly he thought about rescue. By now his father must be puzzled by his failure to return. He could just see him searching the meadow near the deserted cabin. The captain would notice how nervous the horses were. Surely he would see at least one of the bushes on which he had snapped a twig. All he would need would be one sign to show him the direction the raiders had taken. Jim hugged to him the idea that it wouldn't be long before Captain Moore, Simpson and Irish John would come to his rescue.

The Indians must have had the same thought in their minds, for they never once slackened their pace. But the traveling was hard and when dusk fell, Jim figured they had only covered about eight miles.

4. Forced March

The frontier boy had not eaten since breakfast and he felt starved. He was glad when they halted because he thought that at last his captors would give him some parched corn and jerked meat from their knapsacks. It was a shock to Jim when they merely led him down to a stream and let him drink all the water he wanted. At first he thought they were starving him because he was a prisoner. But he soon saw that they had no food in their pouches; they must have been gone from home a long time.

Black Wolf pointed to a thicket of laurel bushes as

their sleeping place. The bearded chief carefully attached a halter around Jim's neck. The boy glared at his captor and said boldly, "I'm no horse."

The Indian glared back scornfully and looped the other end of the strap around his hand. The young braves wrapped themselves in their blankets and stretched out under the laurel. Jim was shoved down next to one of them with Black Wolf close to him on the other side. The boy gagged. He was not only hungry but the Indian smell of sweat and grease made him almost sick.

Rain began to fall in great drops. The night air grew chilly and damp, very different from the earlier heat of the September day. As the rain continued, Jim remembered his father's having predicted it. Well, at least they had finished cutting the corn the day before. The boy was startled. Could it possibly be only yesterday that he had been cutting corn and riding Prince Charlie?

Jim Moore had never been so miserable in all his fourteen years. He longed now not just for his heavy shoes, but for warmer clothes and a blanket. All three Indians were sound asleep and snoring loudly but the captive was wide awake. To ease his loneliness he muttered some of his thoughts aloud. "Crickety, Ma was afraid for me and then I felt something was powerful wrong. Why didn't I turn back to the cabin even if I couldn't have explained it to Pa? And then why in tarnation didn't I manage to kick that young Indian and get up on Trusty and dash away?"

The halter was pressing on his neck. He managed to ease it a trifle and continued, "Blast that chief for seeing me leaving signals and double blast him for not having even any dried food with them. Oh, if only I was back home in the cabin by the fire right now."

Black Wolf stirred and opened one eye to look at the prisoner. Jim stopped his murmuring and his whining thoughts. He made himself start thinking about the way the rescue party had been organized after this same Black Wolf had carried off Mrs. Ingles two years ago. He remembered his father saying, "With Captain Maxwell heading up the search they'll catch the raiders." And that brought to mind the fact that it had taken that party several days to overtake the Indians. So maybe his rescuers would catch up with them next day. At last he fell asleep. His body was so tired that it demanded rest.

It was still dark when he opened his eyes the next morning. His body was stiff from the cold, his back felt like a ramrod. He tried to turn over to relieve the strain, but Black Wolf jerked awake and the young braves sprang to their feet in alarm.

After the smell of them the night before, Jim was amazed to see the Indians plunge into the mountain stream and bathe thoroughly. He was more astonished when they forced him to do the same and then to get dry by exercise. This did help to take some of the kinks out of his spine but it could not make him any less hungry. His stomach was full of grumbling noises and pain.

By daybreak they were on the move again and continued down Tug Creek about two miles and then started climbing straight up the main Tug Ridge. Jim felt his hunger worse now that they were climbing. It was a gnawing pain. All he could think of was the big breakfast he had eaten the day before. It seemed a hundred years ago.

Now they were virtually running downhill. The briers tore at Jim's bare legs. He was still in country where he had hunted with his father and could tell they were heading for Maxwell's Gap. He began to worry what the redskins would do to him there. That was where Captain Maxwell and his group of pursuers had recovered Mrs. Thomas Ingles from Black Wolf. However, they had killed Maxwell there and the gap had been called after him since that time.

Jim asked himself a question under his breath, "Will they kill me to avenge their defeat in that skirmish with the settlers?"

As they approached the gap the Indians grew very excited. The youngest brave kept hissing questions, the other yelled, "Ai, ai," and Black Wolf made fighting motions with his tomahawk. When he saw Jim watching him, the chief gave an evil grin and shouted, "Me chop white man."

"So," Jim thought, "you *were* the murderer of Captain Maxwell."

The bearded chief disappeared into a nearby thicket. Jim thought surely he must be going after other Shawnees waiting in hiding. But he came back alone, carrying a heavy iron object.

In his surprise Jim cried out, "Why, it's a Dutch oven just like the one Ma bakes her bread in."

The boy looked more closely and noticed rust all over it. He muttered, "So you've had that hidden ever since you had to take to your heels after the rescuers licked you here."

The Indians couldn't understand his words but they caught his look of contempt, and a young brave pulled a knife from his belt and made a slashing motion at Jim's lips. The frontier boy had to be silent. He got to thinking that if the settlers had chased the savages successfully before, they could do it again. Maybe at this very moment, rescuers were nearby and would catch up with them. Jim's hopes soared. His heart started beating hard. He turned around now so the Indians couldn't see his face. This time he must not let them know what he was thinking.

Suddenly there was a noise, a scraunchy, creaky, ripping sound, and then a crash. Jim was so excited he could hardly keep from shouting. The rescue party must be very near. Had they been ambushed by other red men or why were they making such a noise?

His captors yanked him flat to the ground. Black Wolf stole stealthily from tree to tree toward the noise. The minutes dragged for Jim. Oh if only it could be his father and rescuers!

"Please God, don't let Black Wolf kill Pa like he did Maxwell." The boy thought it was certainly a good time to pray. If a fellow ever needed help, he did.

He saw Black Wolf crashing carelessly through the bushes, yelling in a triumphant way. Before he reached them he pointed to a tree and showed the braves how one had fallen to the earth and made the noise. Once again his face took on that evil grin as he said mockingly to Jim, "No-o white men."

Jim stood listlessly in his bitter disappointment and the young braves quickly strapped the iron oven to the boy's back. With a wave of his tomahawk, Black Wolf ordered the boy to get going. It was torment, for the leather thongs and straps cut into his skin and the weight of the oven made him put his feet down hard.

Every step was a jolt to his body and he soon bruised his foot on a rocky place. He let out a sharp "Ouch!" and dropped to the ground. The pain was intense. Instantly the young braves circled around him in a mock dance, clutching one foot and howling as if in pain. Black Wolf glared scornfully at him.

He gritted his teeth and by sheer determination got to his feet. He shouted at his tormentors, "All right, savages, you won't get me down."

His determination and his words were brave but after a while he was in such agony he knew he would have to do something about it. He had read that Indians admired a show of spirit. He wiggled out of the straps and dumped the Dutch oven on the ground and stood belligerently with hands on hips. In a loud voice he declared, "I won't carry it any more, I just won't. None of you is toting anything near so heavy."

Jim did not know how many English words Black Wolf might know but he felt sure he would understand his act of defiance.

The chief promptly detached the pack he was carrying and laid it on the ground. He muttered, "Take."

Not believing anyone's load as heavy as his, Jim gladly leaned over to pick up Black Wolf's pack instead of his own. To his amazement he could not even lift it from the ground. He later found out that inside the Indian's blanket were iron cooking kettles which had been hidden with the oven.

Feeling that he'd been tricked, Jim said sullenly, "Yours too heavy" and once again let the braves tie the oven on his back. Now he tried to ignore the pain and think about why rescuers hadn't come after him. Had Black Wolf really removed every mark he had managed to make? Was it because his father, Simpson and Irish John could not leave his mother and the children unguarded back in Abb's Valley? Maybe none of the men over on the Bluestone River could leave their homes to help search.

The boy's hope of sudden rescue dimmed. Maybe he had been a fool to think his father could get to him so soon. But sooner or later the settlers would come after the Shawnee raiders and he would be freed.

Late that afternoon rain began to fall. The young Indian, who looked so like Black Wolf that Jim was certain he was the chief's son, reached over and snatched his hat. This infuriated the frontier boy. He decided to risk a firm stand before the Indians seized his shirt and pants and left him naked. Jim doubled up his fist, struck the young Shawnee a hard blow in the stomach and grabbed back his hat. He yelled, "Leave me alone or I'll bust you one in the face."

The three Indians all looked astonished but did not strike back. Instead the young brave held his gun toward Jim, pointed to the gunlock, cradled his hand over it to cover it, pointed to the hat and again covered the lock, showing that he wished to protect it from the rain. Well, that was a different matter, Jim decided. Reluctantly he returned the hat. He knew it would be taken anyway. The Shawnee grunted but looked less fierce as he took it.

Jim felt better. He had stood up to the Indians and they had not killed him then and there. They had even acted more friendly. That night, just before they lay down to sleep, the rain stopped and Young Wolf handed him back the hat. This really did surprise him.

Lying on wet laurel leaves, Jim twisted and turned with the misery of being cold, wet and hungry. He had a blister on one foot and the other was throbbing from the bad stone bruise. Worst of all was the pain in his stomach. He lay wondering how long a boy could live without food. They had not passed even one persimmon tree from which to pull fruit, and there hadn't been enough frost yet to cure the chestnuts or acorns so humans could eat them.

Jim spoke softly to himself, "If only the red men would travel close to the streams we might sight some small animals. But away up on these ridges we'll never see any. Oh well, they wouldn't shoot if they saw any. That would give 'em away to the rescuers that must be coming. And they sure wouldn't light a fire to cook. That'd be just like a signal."

He woke up stiff and aching and said right out loud, like a declaration of independence, "This is the third day, Shawnees, and that makes it the ninth of September. Before the sun sets they'll be coming to get me back."

Young Wolf cuffed him hard and silenced him. Jim knew that it was useless to strike back. His spurt of courage petered out and he felt lower than before. He

could hardly choke back the tears as he thought what
all the family would be doing in Abb's Valley. His
wonderful Prince Charlie would be frisking around
in the meadow, showing off to the older horses. His
mother, oh his poor mother, would be fixing breakfast
while her heart ached over his capture. But whatever
she was feeling, she would be cooking the usual thick
slices of bacon to feed the ones left at home. Joe was
probably scattering corn to the chickens. Wow, he was
glad Joe hadn't come with him the morning of the
capture.

By the middle of the morning, when rain started
falling, Jim was in agony. But he had to keep going.
He found it helped him to mutter under his breath,
"Keep moving, keep moving. Soon they'll come."

They were moving fast that afternoon, going downhill toward the clear fork of Tug Creek. Suddenly
Jim heard the rattling sound that every frontier boy
dreaded. There was no other noise like that rattle of
the rattlesnake. The boy jerked up short and almost
caused Black Wolf to fall over him. The Shawnee
turned to rearrange his pack and Jim struggled to get
the iron oven off his back to hurl on the snake. He
had no other weapon and the red men were acting as
if they did not even see the coiled-up reptile. When
Black Wolf turned and saw what Jim was about to do,
he seized the captive and pushed him behind him,
and circled the snake, chanting all the while, *"Ne,
cana. Ne, cana, Ne, cana."* He spoke the words in
a rhythm and they seemed to hypnotize the snake.
They moved quickly on. Jim looked back and marveled that the poisonous snake did not move. Was this

a secret power the Indians had? Why hadn't they killed it? Was this a superstition or part of their religion?

Black Wolf chose a projecting cliff that night to protect them from the rain. To Jim's delight he saw the Indians rubbing sticks to create a spark for lighting a fire. But the second he saw a crackling flame leap up in the middle of the twigs his spirits took a dive. The lighting of the fire meant Black Wolf must not any longer fear being overtaken by a rescue party bent on recovering him. But then he saw the chief cut saplings and stick them in the ground with sharpened ends pointed outward to spear anyone who might sneak up in the night. Jim muttered, "He's still not quite sure."

The young braves went to a huge yellow poplar tree standing within the light of the flames. They peeled off the bark near the roots. Returning to the fire, they pounded the strips on a flat stone and tossed it into a kettle Black Wolf had hung over the fire. Now they crouched on their haunches, waiting for the water to boil and draw the essence out of the bark. When it had cooked enough, Black Wolf took the first taste, then the others followed his example. They smacked their lips in appreciation and drank deeply of the bark tea or broth. Finally they offered Jim some and he grabbed it. The hot drink helped the awful pangs of hunger in his stomach. He drank on and on until he felt almost full.

Afterward, lying close to the fire, Jim paid some attention to what the Indians were saying. He heard that word, *meshewa* again and again. So they were still talking about Trusty. Did a horse mean more than anything else to a savage? Would they kill him because they hadn't captured the horse?

When Jim noticed the Indians searching for small game the next morning, he knew they no longer feared a rescue party. Black Wolf had his rifle cocked for game. He was grinning slyly. But even to get a shot, the chief would not give up traveling the high ridges. Once they spied a great bird wheeling and dipping in the distant sky. Jim burst out, "It's an eagle!"

It was not until midafternoon that they sighted anything. But then luckily it was a buffalo. Even Jim had to admire the long shot with which Black Wolf brought it down. The young braves swiftly skinned the big animal and started on the butchering. They took out the paunch of the buffalo and shook it in the stream to wash it. Then cutting it in pieces, they threw these into the iron kettle hanging over the fire.

Jim was so starved that he eyed the raw buffalo meat longingly. He waited until the Indians were busy with the paunch and sneaked over to the buffalo carcass. Not possessing a knife, he tried to yank a piece loose with his bare hands. Instantly he was seized from behind by Black Wolf, who was screaming, "No-o, no-o." The chief smacked Jim in the stomach and then rubbed his own as if in pain and imitated the act of vomiting.

The frontier boy knew that hunters never ate solid food after a long hunger, but the sight of the meat had been too much for him.

Soon the buffalo broth was made and they all drank it greedily. Having it inside him gave Jim the strength to keep slogging along the rest of the afternoon. He fastened his thoughts on the minute when the Indians would broil the buffalo meat and he'd bite into a piece. It couldn't come too soon, for he felt light-headed and dizzy.

When they made camp, Jim patted the meat and said happily, "Going to eat soon now."

But he was doomed to disappointment. The Indians just made more broth. Jim was furious. He shouted at them, "You're just torturing me. Look how skinny I am. I'm going to faint from hunger and I'll probably never wake up again and then you'll have no prisoner to take home."

Black Wolf looked at him stonily. He had not understood the words but he knew the boy wanted the meat. Once again he went through the act of rubbing his stomach and pretending to vomit.

The time came when Jim decided he simply could not stand the pain of the straps holding the oven any longer. They had cut into his back and raised great welts. So he filled the oven with leaves and turned it upside down on his head. This was tiring but at least it did not torture his back.

With that misery partly solved for a while, Jim realized how cold the weather was getting. He never dreamed it would be this much frostier in September up on the mountain tops than back in the sheltered valley he was used to.

It was the day after they had eaten the buffalo broth. The Shawnees had paused for a midday rest. Black Wolf, who had never let the boy get more than a few feet away from him, now sent Jim downhill to a stream below. He had been given the pot to fetch water for cooking.

Jim almost skipped. How wonderful to be away from the Indians even this far. Then a thought hit him and he cried out, "Oh, this means they know there's no chance of my escaping."

He raced down to the stream and crouched under the bank, where he thought he was safe from the eyes of the Indians. He kneeled down and tried to pray but a great burst of tears flooded from his eyes and he was choked with sobs. Finally he was able to say, "Oh God, help me, please. It's terrible now but what's going to happen to me when they get me to their village? If they torture me or burn me at the stake, I don't know whether I can act like a man. I'm so scared. God, please show Pa and his friends where to find me."

And then the tears started again and the sobbing. Finally he got hold of himself and climbed wearily up the bank, carrying the pot of water. When he reached Black Wolf he saw scorn on the chief's face. So the savage had been watching him and had seen him give way to his grief!

The red warrior sneeringly pointed to the tear stains on Jim's face. He shook the tomahawk menacingly over Jim's head and hissed evilly at him. Jim didn't know what his captor was threatening nor did he much care. Things looked bad but he felt better for having said that prayer.

It was a relief to bathe his feet in a cold mountain stream that evening when Black Wolf camped earlier than usual. Then, for the first time, Black Wolf left off the halter around his neck and he was able to sleep better.

One day, two days, three days dragged by before they saw another buffalo. This time Jim spied it first and nudged Young Wolf, who brought it down with a lucky shot. The Indians built a fire and rigged a spit out of green boughs. On this they roasted enough of the meat to eat then. Throwing green boughs on the fire, they smoked the rest to take with them.

From this time on, each morning at sunrise and each night at sunset Black Wolf staged a performance. He drew off to himself, stood very erect, facing the north-west, sucked in a deep breath, and then let out one long, terrifying warwhoop. He made the sound last as long as possible and it reverberated like an echo from any nearby mountain.

Each time Young Wolf came slyly up to the ex-hausted boy, poked a finger into his protruding ribs and imitated the chief giving the yell. He would point tauntingly at Jim, hold up one finger and say, "*Negote*."

"I don't know your Shawnee jabber but any fool could tell your old man is screaming that he's bringing home one captive. Well, I might just fool him. I might just die of starvation or plain misery before he gets me there."

Jim decided Black Wolf must have started worrying about the danger of that very thing, for the bearded man watched him whenever he stumbled from weari-ness. Then the chief slowed the pace.

That night, after soaking his feet in a stream and eating a smoked piece of buffalo, Jim listened to the

Indians trying to decide their exact position. They were lying on their backs staring up at the stars. Over and over they used the word *alagwa*. Jim resolved right then to try to remember that word for star and the others he had picked up. They might help him to escape. There was *gimewane*, for instance. That meant rain. He could say *"Nipe"* for water and *"Scoote"* for fire. His using the expressions had even seemed to amuse his captors. But the massive chief had looked at him murderously the time he had unwisely repeated the word *"meshewa,"* horse. As terrible as he felt, a thrill came over him at the thought that he had kept Black Wolf from capturing Trusty. Thank goodness they hadn't even seen his own Prince Charlie!

Jim continued to drag one foot after another to avoid being poked in his bony ribs by a rifle. His mind was almost a blank. He was startled out of his apathy, one brisk early autumn day, by a whoop. Young Wolf broke out of line and climbed straight up a tall tree. From the top he shouted, *"Kiskepila Sepe."*

The chief's face lit up and he bellowed at Jim as if he were deaf, "O-hio, O-hio, O-hio."

Jim stared back at Black Wolf as if it didn't matter, but inside he felt sick. For across the Ohio River the Shawnees would be safe in their own country.

5. Dangerous Crossing

The sight of the Ohio River made Jim forget his misery. Never had he seen a body of water so big, so powerful. Why, this was no river for fording. How would the Indians cross it? He saw no canoes tied up at the river's edge. But maybe Black Wolf had them hidden somewhere.

Jim stood gazing at the swift currents and eddies. The Indians were busy unloading their packs on the bank. The boy muttered, "Across that we'll come to the Shawnee settlements. Is Black Wolf going to show me off as proof of his scouting raid into Virginia? Will they kill me, or what?"

Black Wolf clapped his great hand over Jim's mouth and pushed him to the ground. He waved the toma-hawk and barked out, "Stay." It was one of the few English words he knew.

Now the chief joined the young braves to search for fallen logs. They dragged these to a flat, grassy place on the high bank. The braves chattered with pleasure and the captive knew that it was because they were nearing home.

Lying on his back, Jim stretched out full length to try to rest his aching, emaciated body. He stared straight up, his mind a blank. Then idly he noticed a strange cloud formation off to the north. "Back home that would mean a storm was brewing."

The Shawnees paid no attention to the sky. They were busy chopping down wild grapevine. Young Wolf slashed away as if he were doing some kind of savage dance. They dragged the vines to the logs and wove them in and out to lash the logs into a sturdy raft.

It took them nearly as long again to fashion several crude paddles out of sizeable logs. Young Wolf also chopped down three slender trees to serve as poles.

Jim watched the black clouds move closer. For the first time, Black Wolf noticed his captive gazing up-ward and turned to look himself. He grunted when he saw the angry clouds and shouted, *"Pasquawke."* The young braves looked quickly at the sky but shook their heads to deny any possibility of a storm.

"They're not going to admit a storm's coming. They're in a hurry to get home," Jim thought.

But they weren't the only ones in a hurry. Black Wolf decided to forget the threatening cloud and gave a sharp command. With Jim adding his feeble strength to that of the Indians, the four of them lowered the raft into the water.

The Virginia boy could hardly believe he was about to cross the mighty Ohio. He remembered a book back home about the early explorers and how both the French and English had claimed this country and fought over it. He recalled Crabbe's accounts at the Poage cabin.

Black Wolf shouted violently at him. Jim came out of his daydream and leaped down from the bank to the small raft. The weight of the Dutch oven made Jim land heavily and Young Wolf growled angrily and thrust a pole into the boy's hands. They started to shove away from shore. Almost instantly the current caught the raft and whirled it around. The bearded chief used his pole with great skill and they began to make progress. Once out of the shallows, the men swapped the poles for the crude paddles.

Black Wolf's powerful muscles rippled as he dug his paddle into the swirling waters and pulled back in great even strokes. Jim worked at it, gaining some strength from the excitement and danger of the crossing. He felt sure the Ohio must be unusually swollen from the rains that had plagued them on the long march. Surely it was not naturally this turbulent. Now a small whirlpool caught them and they strained to pull through the tricky waters. It was grueling work. No one said a word or even grunted, for they needed every ounce of their energy.

Jim felt a sudden change in the air. There was a quick chill, the kind that comes just before a storm. He looked up. The gray cloud was directly overhead and another was approaching it. It was only a matter of minutes before raindrops hit them. An explosion of wrath burst from the lips of Black Wolf. He berated the young braves for having miscalculated the weather. With a mighty effort, the men swung the raft to avoid a whirlpool dead ahead.

The rain soon became a driving downpour. The raft was wet, the paddles slipped in the men's hands. Jim knew that it was a squall and that it would soon be over. Meanwhile, it was impossible to see on the river. They were half way across but the current was very swift. Jim realized they could easily go under. Well, maybe it would be just as well to drown as to be killed on the other side. He looked at the Shawnees. They were straining at their paddles, their heads down.

There was a violent jolt and Young Wolf was hurled off the raft. He had been kneeling and bringing his paddle forward. The impact of a great log, which they had not seen whirling toward them, had thrown him completely off balance.

Instantly Jim grabbed a pole and stuck it out for the young brave to seize. But the current was sweeping the Shawnee downstream. Young Wolf was a powerful swimmer and fought back against the seething river. The three on the raft paddled with all their might. The chief barked out an order and they worked downstream to get below the swimmer. It was easy enough to go down with the current. But then came the tough job of trying to get Young Wolf back up on the raft without turning it over. The Indians had to keep paddling. Jim knew it was up to him to rescue Young Wolf.

Jim stuck the pole out. Twice the Indian lost his grip on it. Once, floating debris almost wrenched the pole from Jim's grip. Finally Young Wolf held on to it and Jim drew him toward the raft. With a massive effort, Jim dragged him up on the crude vessel.

Now began a long struggle to work back upstream. The squall was lessening and the rain was not quite so violent.

It was a weary foursome that landed on the far side of the Ohio. Jim sank to the ground and stretched out, wet as he was. He would never know where he had gotten that sudden spurt of strength to pull Young Wolf out of the water. But now it was completely spent. His teeth were chattering and the chill made his body shake. He wondered why he had made the effort.

Even the skilled Black Wolf had a hard time making a fire. But finally the wet wood caught and the heat dried out captors and captive.

Young Wolf's exuberant spirits returned fast. He included Jim with a good-natured slap on his shoulder. The danger was over and the young brave was headed for home. He danced around the fire yelping, "*Scioto, Scioto.*"

Black Wolf struck his breast and boasted to Jim, "Scioto Shawnee river."

Jim thought bitterly, "Yes, the Scioto is a Shawnee river but the Ohio just came near drowning a Shawnee but you wouldn't thank a mere white boy for pulling him out."

The party started off now in the usual line of march. Jim figured that this much-used trail must lead directly to the Shawnee settlements.

The Indians were in good humor now but became even more so that afternoon when Black Wolf shot a fine buck deer. They skinned and roasted it and ate royally.

Young Wolf leaped up in the air and shouted when they reached the banks of the Scioto. After dumping their packs and making a fire, Black Wolf examined the knives of the young braves.

Instantly Jim expected them to stab him. Had they brought him all this way so they could kill him here on their own river? And then he sagged in relief. Black Wolf was ordering them to carve on a tree. The massive chief stalked off alone into the woods.

Jim huddled by the small fire. His stomach tightened with fear of what was to come. He remembered John Simpson telling of riding a race back in England and saying, "Me belly was pulled as tight as a seaman's knot." And then he recalled that it was the only big race Simpson had ever lost. Jim forced his taut muscles to relax and said to himself, "Well, I don't intend to lose if I can help myself. Not even if Black Wolf does bring back a bunch of screaming Shawnees from wherever he's gone."

He inched toward the young braves to see what they were carving. They ordered him back to the fire. Sitting there in the cold autumn air, a mood of despair swept over him. Nothing less than an armed body of militia could tear him loose from his captors now that they were in Shawnee country. How could he hope for that?

Dusk was falling when Black Wolf returned, carrying a load of ammunition he had earlier cached away somewhere, stolen ammunition, Jim knew. After handing out a few of the bullets to the braves, he studied the carving they had done while he was gone. Grunting, he added a few swift strokes of his own and ordered Jim to come and look. It was crude but there was no denying its meaning. On one side there were three big men and on the other a thin figure, a boy. There was a line or rope between the two. Jim gave no indication that he understood, but well he knew it was a record of his capture. Why did they do this? Could they be establishing proof just before they killed him?

The boy felt himself going cold again. It was as if something was jerking inside his stomach. He had stood so much on this nightmare of a trip. He wasn't sure he could bear up against what lay ahead.

Nothing happened that night and the Indians took the trail again the next morning. After a short march, they stopped. Shaking some gunpowder from their deerskin pouches, they mixed it with hunks of the dark brown earth. Then they wet it and stirred it into a thick black paste. They smeared the mixture over their faces and in streaks down their throats. Jim forced himself to stare at them and to show no surprise at their hideous, sinister appearance.

Now Black Wolf darted toward the boy and yanked off the scrap of grapevine with which he had tied his hair back off his shoulders. During the weeks they had been on the trail, Jim's yellow hair had grown very long.

This act scared Jim even more than the paint on the men's faces. Were they preparing to scalp him and carry the scalp victoriously into the village to present to the tribal chief?

The Indians hurriedly strapped on their packs and started off in a big rush. The path was well worn and the raiders moved swiftly.

Jim felt sure the men would not have blackened themselves unless they meant to kill him. He was in an agony of mind. He believed he could face death without acting too badly, but he was desperately afraid of proving a coward if they tortured him. How could a fellow know what he would do when that awful pain began? He struggled to shake off the terror of torture.

There was the smell of smoke in the air, and there were small paths branching out from the main trail. Jim knew they were approaching a settlement. Young Wolf was counting aloud as they moved swiftly forward. Like a drumbeat he barked out the numbers. Jim counted. The Indian stopped at twenty-two, for they had been on the march twenty-two days.

Through the trees Jim could see a corn field—the corn stacked in shocks just as in Abb's Valley. A great lump welled in his throat. Back home they would be shucking the corn he had helped to cut. He knew that life would be going on in Abb's Valley even though the family ached with grief over his capture. The sun would rise, the sun would set, with chores performed, stock cared for, meals prepared. His father would carry on his horse-raising but his face wouldn't look the same. His mother would try to dull her fears by working until she fell into bed at night sufficiently exhausted to sleep and so, for a brief spell, blot out her anguish over him. His poor colt, Prince Charlie, was probably being neglected in his absence. No one would have time for really careful training.

Now Black Wolf had led them around the corn field. They were within a thousand feet of the village. To the left lay a flat field, beaten down hard as if by constant use. Could it be for drilling? No, Indians didn't fool with that. Maybe war dances? Ahead Jim could make out a sizeable collection of homes. They were like rounded huts but not built of logs. In the center was a very large structure, constructed in the same manner as the huts, and to its side was a hut of medium size. The village was well laid out with lanes between the huts. Smoke rose from nearly all the dwellings.

But Black Wolf had halted and was preparing himself for one of his long whoops. He drew himself to his full height and expanded his chest like a bellows. The great shout served as an announcement of triumphant return.

Instantly any number of boys and dogs emerged from the village and raced across the meadow toward them. Black Wolf ignored them. He walked stiffly along the hard-beaten path that led to the village entrance, where a crowd was gathering.

The braves stood in front, some old, some young.

Black Wolf's whoop had interrupted them in some ordinary daily task and so they were not elaborately dressed. They wore deerskin kilts supported by belts just below their waist lines. Some wore shirts of skin, others were bare above the waist. Behind the men hovered the squaws and young maidens.

An older man, who had taken time to put on a ceremonial skullcap mounted with feathers, now passed through the crowd and stood in front of his people. He raised his hand in official greeting.

Black Wolf poured out a stream of words. Jim could understand few of them, but he could not miss the violent curiosity of the crowd. They stared at him and nudged each other.

The speech was over. The crowd surged forward. The braves congratulated Black Wolf and the women surrounded Jim, fingering his long, fair hair, staring into his blue eyes. They lifted up shreds of his shirt to look at the white skin underneath and then pointed to the scratches that covered his bare legs. Boys pushed through the crowd of women and felt the muscles in the captive's arms. Jim ached to haul off and punch them but he grimly forced himself to pretend he noticed nothing.

A tall boy lifted Jim's hair above his head and yelled "Ai, ai." At that moment Jim would have swapped his beloved colt for a knife with which to kill the Indian youth and then whack off this long yellow hair he had grown on the trip.

He remembered now that his mother and Mary often spoke of his being "well favored as to looks." He hoped fervently that the Indians wouldn't think so. That would make him too choice an object for the tomahawk or scalping knife.

The chief, with the feathers in his skullcap, raised his voice. The crowd reluctantly broke up. There was one elderly man who had stood aside throughout the crowd's inspection of the captive.

This old man, who had a high-domed head, looked at Jim and then gave Black Wolf a piercing stare before turning on his heels and going back to the village.

To the lad's surprise he was not led straight into the Indian town. Black Wolf stood talking, in heated tones, to a woman older than he. The squaw was tall like Wolf and somewhat resembled him. The two young braves approached the man who had led them on the raid. Without even looking at them he waved them toward the village. The pair immediately ran toward the group of young maidens, who were looking with admiration at them.

Jim's captor pulled him away from the lingering onlookers. Followed by the tall old squaw, whom he called Wapeuttequah, the three made their way to a rather large hut, or wigwam, located in a grove just north of the village. The woman lifted the flap over the opening and Black Wolf bent over to enter.

There was a bony, emaciated old man sitting on the far side of the fire. He looked at Black Wolf through narrowed eyes and raised his hand in greeting.

Jim's captor muttered, "Muga."

The squaw and Black Wolf sat close to the fire, their voices rising and falling. They were arguing about something, Jim could tell by their tones. The squaw's husband took no part in the conversation but sat silently puffing on a long-stemmed pipe. If he had any opinion on whatever was being discussed by his wife and Black Wolf, he kept it to himself.

Jim looked around the wigwam. Poles or stakes had been stuck in the ground in a big circle. They must have been placed there, he noted, when they were green and full of sap, for they had been bent without cracking. Where they met at the top, the poles were tied together with thongs of leather. Then other smaller poles had been attached to make the side framing.

To the framing, mats had been attached. The overhead mats were made of the bark of trees. Jim had often helped his father skin bark off trees when the sap was up and then press it down flat by laying heavy timbers on it, so he knew that was what the Indians had done to make this rainproof roof. The mats that were bound to the sides of the wigwam were of reeds neatly woven together and formed almost windproof walls.

Against these walls a raised platform was built about a foot above the bare, hard-beaten earth floor. The platform was between six and eight feet wide and covered with bearskins, neatly stretched out. On the very top lay deerskins, which the boy guessed the Indians used as blankets.

Jim looked at the squaw's bony old husband and wondered if he had been strong enough to split the trees that were the base for the platform. The two elderly people appeared to live here alone, but maybe they had a son who was now gone away. The man Black

Wolf had called Muga saw Jim looking at him. With an almost imperceptible movement the old fellow signaled the captive to stretch out on the platform at the far side of the wigwam. He handed him a bowl of cold hominy.

The next morning when Jim woke from a sleep of exhaustion, Black Wolf and the squaw were again seated by the fire. Wapeuttequah rose from time to time and went to a pile of goods stacked against the wall. First she showed Black Wolf a handful of silver brooches but the raider shook his head. Her next offering was a bundle of mink skins, dark brown and glossy. Jim's captor stroked the pelts a minute.

The boy watched his captor's face. Black Wolf was evidently tempted by these skins. Jim knew the two had been bargaining for something, and he felt quite sure that he was the thing being traded.

"*Meshewa*," Black Wolf yelled out in a provoked way. "*Meshewa, meshewa*."

"He wants to trade me for a horse," Jim decided and groaned to himself, "Oh, why didn't I let them capture Trusty back in Abb's Valley? Does my whole life have to hang on horses?"

Wapeuttequah was glaring defiantly at Black Wolf and shaking her head.

Black Wolf leaped to his feet, his face a thundercloud, angrier than Jim had ever seen him. He spat into the fire, put his hand on the knife thrust into his belt, and strode furiously out of the wigwam.

6. Shawnee Trial

The following days were a nightmare of suspense to
Jim. Momentarily he expected his captor to return
and take him away. He could hardly force himself to
swallow the hominy and scraps of smoked fish that the
squaw gave him. The second day the squaw brought in
several armfuls of corn and indicated he could husk
and shell it. The work was a relief after the long hours
of just sitting.

When he had been cooped up like this for three
days, Jim could hear a big commotion in the village.
The squaw heard it too and spoke to her husband.

Wapeuttequah went to her pile of belongings and
pulled out an elaborately beaded skirt and a soft deerskin
blouse. It was ten shades lighter than the dirty one she
had on. The woman retired into the dark portion of the
wigwam to dress. Her husband put on a kilt of beauti-
fully cured buckskin and then wrapped himself in a
cloak or great cape of skins. The cloak had been hanging
on a hook but covered with a ragged blanket. Jim's eyes
popped when he saw that the cape was made entirely of
matched skins, the pelts of small animals such as squirrels, beavers and muskrats. Muga drew it around him as
if the warmth of it comforted him.

At this moment Black Wolf shouted at the wigwam
entrance and lifted the flap. He shouted out the word
"*Shemanese*," the term Shawnees used for any American. Jim went outside to face his captor, who was
dressed in ceremonial grandeur. On his head he wore
a skullcap made out of green wands and from this
stuck up and hung down the back nine exploit feathers, each a tail feather of the golden eagle.

The bearded man had removed the black paste from
his face but streaked it with brighter hues. His great
bronze chest was bare except for massive necklaces of
bears' claws. His deerskin kilt was not only clean but
handsomely embroidered around the bottom, as were
the new moccasins on his feet.

Black Wolf marched the captive straight toward
the entrance to the village, up the main lane to the
huge wigwam or council house. The first person Jim
noticed in the crowd already gathered there was the
old man with the high-domed head who had stared at
him and his captor the day they had reached the

village. To the boy's amazement the elderly fellow was now dressed even more resplendently than Black Wolf. A small cape or shawl made entirely of birds' feathers thrown around his shoulders obviously marked him as a man of position within the tribe.

All the people of the village had put on their finest apparel for this event, and they made a colorful and frightening group. A wiry, elderly man, who held himself like an arrow, was called on to begin the proceedings. As he talked, he made great sweeping motions and then started chanting a series of syllables, "*Matche-ma-ne-too.*" His voice rose and fell in a rhythm as he stamped about the council house and glided toward the open door. During this performance the other Indians kept their eyes lowered. From stories he had heard, Jim figured this must be the medicine man driving out the bad spirits. He knew now that he was going to be subjected to some kind of trial before his fate was decided.

The medicine man stood in the doorway making welcoming gestures and bowing low. As he rose his dark eyes flashed with excitement and he began sonorously chanting a new word, "*Weshe-ma-ne-too.*" The sound filled the council house.

Finally the chanter straightened his body to its fullest height and in a crescendo of sound, shouted "*Ne-we-cane-tepa, Weshemanetoo,*" and lifted his hands high above his head.

From the expressions on the faces of the crowd, Jim decided that the Bad Spirit had been driven out and the Good Spirit persuaded to come in.

Now the presiding chief motioned to an elder of

the tribe, who left his position by the wall and stood
to face the assembly. As this first speaker droned on
and on, Jim looked around at the people who would
judge him. Was there one friendly face in the crowd?
Did they all hate him, hate him because he was one
of the white people moving in on land their fore-
fathers had hunted over?

The boy studied the chief of the village. His face
was like a blank wall. It showed no feeling. Jim could
not guess what way he would vote, or was he too
important to vote on a mere American boy?

The chief signaled for the two young braves who
had accompanied Black Wolf and they replaced the
elder, who solemnly went back to his place by the
wall. The youngest brave spoke first. He did not seem
as sure of himself as he had on the trail. He kept looking at Black Wolf to see if he was pleasing him. Now
he was growing more bold as he talked about
"*Kiskepila Sepe.*" He could brag about the crossing
of the Ohio because he had paddled like a maniac and,
at the same time, had stayed on the raft.

It was Young Wolf's turn. He was exuberant as
usual. The glowing tones of his voice made whatever
he was saying sound full of success. After a great
torrent of words he pointed to his father, Black Wolf,
and raised his right hand high in tribute. The youth
held his head high to show off his one exploit feather,
and then bowed as his father was summoned forward
to speak.

Black Wolf swelled out his chest and began to talk.
Jim, who had become accustomed to the behavior of
his captor, decided the powerfully muscled warrior

was boasting. Every now and then he would puff out his cheeks and glare at the captive. Each time he did that, silence became complete in the council house and the assembled Shawnees turned and stared at the fourteen-year-old American.

As he spoke, Black Wolf grew more hot-tempered, shaking his fist in war-like motions and shouting, "*Meshewa, tepawa meshewa.*" To Jim, the bearded man seemed obsessed with horses. He was forever talking about them.

The raider's fierceness was taking effect. Some of the young braves jumped up and down and shouted approvingly "Ho," or "Ha," and others turned to one another, rolling out the word "*meshewa.*" The warriors milled about the council house as if ready for a war dance. Jim felt the breath drain out of him. He gasped from the heat and stench in the room.

The presiding chief looked puzzled as if he did not know what to think. A number of older warriors looked painfully solemn. One violently excited man, whose eyes had a wild gleam, kept asking with a question mark in his voice, "*Shemanese meaneleh?*"

Jim's heart sank. He didn't like the look of that man. He knew he meant him harm. Jim well knew that the word *Shemanese* referred to him, the American. He decided this wild appearing warrior was trying to turn the talk from future raids to the immediate issue of disposing of him.

He succeeded in this, for another man said gruffly, "*Shemanese,*" and pointed straight at Jim.

The presiding chief nodded and signaled for quiet. Jim's hands and feet dripped with nervous sweat.

His chances didn't look very good. He tried to keep his body absolutely still and his face stern and unafraid. He must not reveal his feelings.

To his surprise, the captive saw the withered old man who had stared at him at the time of his arrival rise to speak. The elderly man pushed back his feather cape and raised his hand above his head with authority. The motion hushed even the wild mutterings of the warrior with the fanatic look.

The ancient chief spoke with quietness but power. He had the gift of oratory. At first his eyes had a far-off look. Every now and then the saga was interrupted by quiet ho's and ha's mouthed by the older braves.

After a long stretch, the old voice saddened and the speaker looked at Black Wolf and some of the other more cruel-faced warriors and petty chiefs gathered in the council house. Though old, the orator could give to his words the impact of bullets. He flourished his tomahawk and repeatedly brought it down in the scalping motion.

Then, unexpectedly, the old chief dropped his voice to a dramatic whisper. He pointed directly to Jim Moore and Black Wolf. The aged speaker sounded deeply sorrowful. He swept his arm around the council room to indicate all his people and then lifted his eyes pleadingly to heaven and, in a rising tone, called *"Weshemanetoo."* Jim hoped the Good Spirit was listening.

The people seemed stirred. The older chiefs were looking oddly at Black Wolf.

The orator again switched tactics and his voice boomed out, reminding Jim of his father reading prophecies from the Old Testament. The boy became convinced that the old chief was predicting what would happen in the future. His tone was grim and full of warning. Finally the speaker folded his arms across his chest and, in silence, looked at his fellow Shawnees. The speech was over. There was no exaltation on the old man's face, only the look of one who has done a hard duty.

The presiding chief immediately called for the decision as to the disposition of the captive. He raised his hands a short way and then pointed to two braves and nodded his head up and down in a solemn way. The men disappeared to come back quickly, bearing woven mats piled with grains of yellow corn. They stood by the presiding chief holding the stiff mats out in front of them at breast level. The chief raised his hands again and pointed to two older braves. They disappeared and promptly returned with two wooden bowls, elaborately carved.

Still inscrutable as to expression, the chief intoned the words, "*Skillewaythetha Shemanese—nepwa,*" and stared at Jim.

Then in a rising tone, he said, "*Da-me,*" and waved his hand imperiously to the corn held on high by the braves.

The two men moved majestically among the crowd. Each person, who had the right to vote, ceremoniously picked up one grain of corn.

The chief ordered the older braves holding the empty bowls to circulate; the chief repeated that word "*nepwa.*" Jim's whole body was like ice. He had heard Black Wolf shout out that word whenever they had killed an animal on the trail. The boy forced himself to watch a group of fierce-looking braves drop their grains of corn into the bowl that would mark him for death. He felt a wave of nausea sweeping through his body and turned aside to draw in deep breaths to fight it.

Now the braves had returned the *nepwa* bowl to a spot at the chief's feet and taken up the other bowl. The presiding officer once again raised his hand and intoned, *"Skillewaythetha Shemanese—lenawawe."*

They circulated this bowl. Jim watched eagerly now. Yes, a great many seemed still to have the grain of corn in their hands. Solemnly they dropped it in the bowl. It looked like many grains to Jim but he was too nervous to feel sure.

The presiding chief summoned three of the oldest men in the council house to him and pointed at the bowls. They proceeded to count the grains. The old chief with the feather cape who had spoken rose to report. He said, in his fine resonant voice, *"Lenawawe."* The presiding chief called to Black Wolf and pointed to Jim.

The boy's captor seized him by his neck and pushed him toward the chieftain, who looked at him solemnly for a moment and then, speaking to the crowd, rang out the words, *"Shemanese—lenawawe."* He nodded his head to Black Wolf, who promptly marched his captive out of the council house.

The Virginian was desperate to know what they had voted. They had voted against death, but did that word *lenawawe* mean torture? He had never heard it before.

Black Wolf almost raced him back to the wigwam. Wapeuttequah came panting after them. The boy thought he detected a gleam of anticipated pleasure in the face of the tall old woman, but she merely pointed to the platform where he had slept before.

Jim's imagination ran wild now as he tried to figure out what they might do to him. Would they start that night or the next morning? Black Wolf suddenly dropped down by the fire, as did the squaw. They were arguing and bargaining again. The woman interrupted the talk only long enough to reach over and throw Jim a badly worn bearskin. The boy was exhausted, drained of energy now that the tense scene in the council house was over. If these two were planning torture, they would not start on it until the morrow. He'd better try to get some rest to face the horror that he had so long dreaded. The unhappy captive finally drifted off to a sleep made miserable by a nightmare of being burned at the stake.

The next morning the squaw seemed full of determination. She handed Jim a wooden bowl filled with corn mush which he forced himself to eat although it was tasteless and cold. Again Black Wolf and the squaw started their conversation. This endless talk was getting on the boy's nerves. He felt like screaming, "Do something, just don't squat there talking." He watched the two warily; Black Wolf was getting angrier and angrier. Suddenly he jumped to his feet and shouted, "*Meshewa!*" It was like a clap of thunder.

Jim groaned, "Oh, if they would only stop shouting horse and just kill me instead and have done with it."

Wapeuttequah rose clumsily and said in a low,

resigned voice, *"Meshewa."* Then she lifted the flap over the entrance to the wigwam and vanished into the chill October morning.

Every nerve in Jim's body was taut. Something was about to happen. Soon the squaw returned and summoned Black Wolf and Jim outside.

She was holding, by a beaded bridle, an old gray horse. Now, like an act in a ceremony, she handed the bridle to Black Wolf whose eyes began to gleam. He stared possessively at the horse.

The squaw said sharply, *"Shemanese."*

Black Wolf, without taking his eyes off the horse, seized Jim's shoulder and pushed him toward the Indian woman. He never even looked at the boy he had captured, but mounted the horse and rode away.

Wapeuttequah pointed to Jim and then to herself and curled up her hand as if she were holding something. The gesture left no doubt. The squaw now owned him—to have and to hold. Black Wolf had sold him for the horse. That was what had been going on.

Jim could not stifle the thought, "I am worth one old horse that my father wouldn't even keep. I guess having that horse will keep the braves from taunting Black Wolf for not capturing Trusty on his raid into Virginia."

7. Squaw's Slave

And so Jim Moore began his life among the Shawnees. He was now a slave, but at least he was alive. He lay under the bear skin and said aloud as many hopeful old sayings as he could remember. "Where there's life there's hope" was one he recalled from his mother. Others were "Where's there's a will there's a way," and his father's remark, "Brave men know what it is to be scared but they never give up. They count on God."

Gradually a little courage seeped back into the tired

boy. He muttered fiercely, "Somehow, sometime, I'll find a way to get out of here and get home."

He became consumed with eagerness to learn more Shawnee words so he could figure out what had happened. Gradually, by listening, he learned that the old chief had pleaded not to kill him. The aged one had that day in the council house told the whole history of the tribe, of their many migrations, their having once lived in the south close to salt water. The orator had spoken of how the Great Spirit had guided the Shawnee people and been good to them. He had warned of the brutal raids Black Wolf and his type of Shawnee had been making against the white people. He had said that raids like that would bring much trouble to the Shawnees, for the white men would come to avenge themselves and kill and burn. Finally the old chief had pleaded with his people to leave the white settlers alone and, as a token, to spare the life of this boy.

Jim was glad that, at least for the time being, his life had been spared. But he suspected that if the Shawnees became angry with him or at acts of white settlers anywhere, they would turn and do away with him.

The squaw began training her slave by taking him to the woods with her for kindling. She stood over him and saw that he gathered sticks that lay on the ground and broke dried bushes. When they returned to the wigwam each time she pointed to the heavy flap of woven reeds that hung over the opening. With her hand, she signaled to him to raise the flap for her that she might enter. Jim Moore knew what she was really making clear was, "Remember you are my slave now and you are here to wait on me."

After some days of only using him to bring in kindling, Wapeuttequah one morning pointed to the fire, which was very low. Then picking up an axe from a pile of tools that lay against the wall of the wigwam, she felt the edge of the steel head. Smiling with pride, she pronounced the word *"Shemanese."*

Jim had to choke back a snort. She did not need to tell him it was American. He wondered from what poor settler's cabin it had been stolen. Perhaps some brave had even used it to bash a white person's brains. There was a possibility that his owner had gotten it by trading furs or skins for it, but Jim doubted it.

The squaw marched him deeper into the woods than they had been before. Besides the axe she carried a rough stone tomahawk to use in case he tried to run away. When they reached a long-fallen tree, she handed him the axe and took up her position close by, with the tomahawk gripped firmly in her right hand. Slave though he was, Jim could not help a wry smile at the tall old woman threatening him in this way when she had just equipped him with a sharp axe. Never once, while he worked, did his owner take her eyes off him.

Back in the wigwam, the squaw hung an iron pot over the fire. She set Jim to husking and shelling dried ears of corn. Then she showed him how she liked the corn cracked on a big flat stone. As fast as he cracked the corn, Wapeuttequah tossed it into the boiling water.

On the way in from the woods, a young brave had passed them returning from his traps. He had rabbits and Wapeuttequah had traded a nice lot of the wood Jim had chopped for one rabbit. Jim had always heard that Indian men loved to hunt but hated to do work. This seemed to bear that out.

Jim watched with interest as the squaw swiftly skinned and cleaned the rabbit and speared it onto a spit over the fire. She ordered Jim to keep turning the spit to cook the meat.

The smell of the cooking made Jim hungrier than ever. He had been fed each day but very meagerly. The squaw, kneeling down by the fire, noticed the starved look in the boy's eyes. To Jim's delight, the woman went outside to her storehouse-leanto and returned with a small pumpkin. She cut this up and put it on to boil in another pot.

When the food was just about cooked, there was a stomping outside the wigwam and Wapeuttequah's husband came in. The old warrior Muga paid no attention to Jim. He went straight to the fire and sat down. The squaw promptly served him his food. The woman saw that her husband was entirely satisfied before she took anything for herself. At last she dished out her own bowl and filled a badly cracked one with food for Jim. She signaled him to sit back at a distance from the fire. Once more Jim was reminded that he was her slave and must keep his position.

The October night was cold and the old squaw felt the chill. She pulled a shawl around her and turned to signal Jim, who was sitting on the platform, his legs stuck straight out in front of him. His feet were turned up. The squaw noticed the horrible sores on the bottoms of his feet. Her eyes narrowed but she signaled the boy to replenish the fire.

Having fetched the wood, Jim crawled back up on the platform to enjoy the warmth in the wigwam, or *wigwa*, as Wapeuttequah called it. The old warrior was crouched by the fire, smoking his pipe and looking as if he were dreaming of hunts he had made. The boy had often seen that look on men back home when they thought back to the pleasures of the chase.

The fire was built in the center of the wigwam and, all during supper, the smoke had gone straight up and out the hole at the top. But all of a sudden the wigwam was filled with smoke. The wind had changed and was blowing gray clouds down the opening.

The old warrior was roused from his pipe-smoking reverie. He barked out the word *"Wunnau-chi-co-mock"* and rolled his eyes upward to the smoke hole.

The squaw seized Jim by the shoulder and pushed him ahead of her out of the wigwam. The outside seemed especially dark after the bright flames of the fire. Wapeuttequah was groping around the sides of the wigwam. Now she called, *"Shemanese."*

Jim stepped closer and she steered his hands to a long rope fashioned out of grapevines. She pressed hard on his hands to make him pull it. He yanked too hard, perhaps, because a shout of disgust rang out from inside the wigwam.

The Indian woman made him do it again and the shouting stopped. Jim was impressed that these people out in the woods had rigged up a mat which they could pull into position to shield the roof hole from wind.

By his second pull he had gotten the shield adjusted to the shift of the wind. Now it wouldn't blow the smoke back down into the wigwam.

Back inside, where the air had cleared, Jim had a sudden new respect for these people whom he had been brought up to consider absolute savages. So they did know something about making a home comfortable.

From the village, occasional shouts had been heard all evening. Now the noises sounded louder and more constant.

Muga reached up to a peg and took down his match-coat. Jim wondered if the old fellow had shot or trapped all the animals whose matching skins made the cloak.

Wapeuttequah signaled to Jim to raise the door flap and the captive boy watched as the aging man headed for the village.

Now the squaw went over to one of her piles of belongings. She grunted with pleasure as she handled each thing. She called sharply, *"Shemanese."*

Jim went to her and she stretched out between them three embroidered mats of deerskin. The squaw pointed to the stitching and then to her own hands. The work was very beautiful. Since he had made up his mind to make friends with this woman who owned him, the tall lad pointed to the embroidery and clapped his hands. It had the desired effect. Wapeuttequah was pleased. He smiled and the squaw smiled back at him.

She stood hugging one of the embroidered mats to her and then started chattering out orders that the boy could not understand until she pushed him toward the wall of the wigwam and motioned to him to hang the decorated mats. As he worked, he could not help wondering why she had not had them up before. Maybe owning a slave had made her feel suddenly rich and she no longer had to hide her wealth.

Jim Moore ran his fingers along the bead embroidery and leaned close to peer at it. He imagined it told the story of a hunt, but the fire did not cast enough light for him to see clearly. Wapeuttequah watched him intently and then called him over to another pile of belongings. She rummaged through the things and murmured, "Ho." Straightening up from her crouching position, she threw a buckskin shirt at Jim.

He caught it and held the garment up before the fire. It was very old and had received much wear so it must have been used by her husband. But now it was too big for the old warrior, who had begun to shrivel up.

The squaw said, *"Shemanese,"* in a kindly tone. So Jim pulled the fringed Indian shirt over his head. The sleeves were too short for his arms but at last he had something to protect him against the wind. His own coarse cotton shirt was in tatters. Now he could throw away the rags.

The old woman pushed him down by the fire and crouched nearby. She was looking at his feet. He looked at them himself and marveled that those two calloused, scratched, bruised feet had brought him over all that rough country from Virginia to this Shawnee village on the headwaters of the Mud River, not far from the Scioto. The feet were still bare and in wretched condition.

Wapeuttequah jerked her thumb to order Jim to stick his feet closer for her to see. She began an ex-

amination of them. Jim hated for her to touch him.
Her bony hands were like claws, but when she felt
the worst places on his feet she was not rough. Her
face showed concern and she even sucked in her breath
as if in sympathy for his misery. Suddenly she pulled
her feet out of her moccasins and stuck them out before
him as much as to say, "That is the way feet ought to
look."

Once more she went to a pile of belongings and came
back with several pouches and a woven basket. She
shook dried leaves out of the pouches and selected several dried roots from the basket. She tossed them together into the kettle of water simmering over the fire.

Jim sat watching her. She was absorbed in brewing
medicine out of herbs the way her people had since the
beginning of time. The old squaw chanted softly to
herself as she stirred the kettle. Her eyes were shut
tight. After a long while she leaned over and sniffed
the brew. She looked like a witch and made the boy
think of Irish John, who was always talking about
witches.

Now the squaw ordered the boy to lift the kettle off
the cleft stick over the fire. Once again she closed her
eyes and stirred the brew to cool it. Suddenly she
stopped and forcibly stuck Jim Moore's two feet into
the big pot. It was all the boy could do to keep from
howling. The herb mixture was scalding. But after the
first shock had passed he could feel the medicine drawing on the sore places. The boy had a dreadful
thought—how could he be sure the squaw knew what
she was doing? She was no medicine man. She might
make his feet worse. He started to draw them out of

the kettle. Wapeuttequah blazed with anger and pushed them back into the solution. Then she shook her hand in his face and disappeared out of the wigwam.

The woman returned with a kettle of cold water. To Jim's horror, he was made to shift his feet from the steaming pot straight into the icy water she had brought. After a few minutes she signaled him to hold his feet near the fire to dry. It had been a violent treatment, but already his feet felt better.

Now from outside the wigwam came the sound of loud voices. The old warrior lifted the entrance flap and stood in the opening with his thin body drawn up as straight as he could get it. He said in a loud, solemn voice, "*Weshe-cat-weloo, kewesthe-laway-pa.*"

Muga always made quite a ceremony out of his goings and comings, acting as though he were reminding his wife that he was still boss in that wigwam. In the days to come, Jim was to get used to him and his sayings. He soon learned that "*Weshe-cat-weloo, kewesthe-laway-pa*" meant "Let us always do good," and that the older Shawnees loved to address each other in those words.

Behind the old warrior, standing in the wigwam entrance, somebody was giggling. A thick-voiced man was talking but kept interrupting himself by silly giggles. The squaw's husband remained standing until the foolish talk died away. Then he strode into the wigwam and fastened his eyes on the white captive. He snapped out the words "fire water," pronouncing the English word like "watah." There was contempt in his voice.

Even though the pronunciation was strictly Shawnee, the words had been English, the first Jim had
heard for so very long. However, he understood the
reason Muga had used them—to blame the white man
for selling fire-water to the young braves and making
them act like idiots, chattering and giggling.

That was the most comfortable night's sleep Jim
had had since he was captured. The sores on his feet
didn't throb as hard, thanks to the squaw's medication.

Bright and early the squaw ordered her slave about
his duties. She had him cut and stack firewood and
bring water from the nearby spring. She made him
carry the bearskins and deerskins out into the bleak
autumn sunlight. After that he was required to brush
out the wigwam with a broom of switches. All the time,
Wapeuttequah sat by the fire patching a worn pair of
moccasins. Finally the mending was done and the
squaw threw the footwear to Jim.

The boy had been hoping that the moccasins might
be for him but he had tried not to count on it. They
had evidently been worn by the squaw, for they were
decorated just like the ones she had on. But what did
he care? They would be some protection for his poor
feet.

The squaw now ordered Jim to follow her, and they
set off through a meadow to some cleared land on the
bank of a creek.

Wapeuttequah spoke to other women of the village
who were already working there. The young American felt ashamed. Here he was, as tall as a man and
strong, yet his owner was only going to use him to do
woman's work. It was with a heart full of resentment

that he worked alongside of the squaw gathering pumpkins off the vines. He carried the pumpkins back to the leanto his owner had near the wigwam. They were stored along with turnips and potatoes in a deep hole in the earthern floor. The vegetables were covered with dirt—just the way his mother kept her root cellar back home in Abb's Valley. Corn and strings of onions hung from the ceiling, but the supply looked very small to Jim when he thought how much his family put away for a winter's use.

Each time that Jim returned from the field to the leanto storage, he passed young Indian braves enjoying some kind of game or sport. He observed as much of it as he could.

There was a bare field right by the village and on it were playing two groups of Shawnee youths. They were all barefooted and seemed bent on only one thing, kicking a funny, flattened-out ball down the field. After several trips in which he passed the field, Jim figured that one group was trying to kick the ball the length of the field and make it pass between two crossed poles set up there. The other side was trying to do the same thing in the opposite direction.

Jim Moore had never seen football before. In fact he had never seen this many young people together before. Back home in Abb's Valley he had a handball but this game was much more exciting than just pitching.

The lithe, swift youths kept rushing down the field. They grabbed each other in flying tackles. There was a constant shouting of "Ai, ai."

The scene was more stirring because the small boys of the village ran up and down the side of the field piping on hollow reeds. This piping was shrill and high and somehow stimulated a person. It made Jim think of Irish John and his one and only possession, a cornet, on which he loved to blow. This Indian piping, however, was much wilder than that produced by the Irishman.

Even with his sore feet, Jim longed to rush out on the field and join in the sport. However, he had watched too long and Wapeuttequah was shouting at him. His owner was much aggravated and spoke sharply to him.

On his last trip of the day to bring in pumpkins, Jim passed the players as they were coming off their field. Young Wolf was one of them. He saw Jim looking at the ball and threw it to him. It was made of buckskin and was about ten inches in diameter. Where it had been laced together, another piece of hide kept the stuffing from coming out. Jim punched the ball and figured out that it was stuffed with moss. Young Wolf promptly grabbed it back from him and ran fast to overtake his fellow players.

Jim's owner again that night examined his feet and made him go through the painful hot and cold soakings.

There was a peculiar bustle going on in the wigwam as Jim stirred under the bearskin coverings. Wapeuttepuah was chatting with her husband. This in itself was unusual as they talked little together. Suddenly the conversation stopped and his owner yelled, "*Shemanese.*"

Jim rose and shook himself. He woke up each morning still exhausted. He was immediately ordered to build up the fire and as soon as the bowl of breakfast mush had been eaten he was signaled outside. The squaw brought hot coals to place under green wood she had required Jim to cut the day before. She speared strips of fresh meat on sharp sticks and rigged them to catch the smoke. Jim was shown how to turn them until the meat was fully jerked or cured.

The old warrior emerged and started sharpening his axe. He seemed happy for the first time since Jim had arrived. When Muga got his long rifle and started cleaning it, Jim knew that the preparations were for a hunt.

Wapeuttequah next set Jim to shelling and parching corn. He filled two skin pouches with the yellow grains for the old warrior to take on the hunt. After they were filled, the squaw set before him other containers and ordered him to continue with the corn and showed him where to store it in her leanto.

In the early afternoon, the old man laid out all the things he would take on his hunting journey. Every item seemed to please him and, to Jim's amazement, Muga went so far as to pat his wife's shoulder in approval of her preparations. Then he signaled Jim to pick up some unshucked ears of corn. He did the same and slung his gun over his shoulder. He led the American lad to the nearby meadow and made it clear that Jim was to throw the corn in the air while he tested his marksmanship. Muga was a good shot but his aim was no longer perfect, for his hands shook a little. However, after he managed to hit the flying ears of corn five times, the old warrior was pleased with himself and, in a burst of good will, handed the gun to Jim. To the boy's amazement, the old fellow trotted down the field and himself threw an ear into the air in a snaking, crooked motion. Jim had not been trained by his father for nothing. He easily exploded the flying object.

The thin old chap threw an ear much farther away and again Jim hit it. Muga exclaimed, "*Ai.*" To Jim it sounded as if he were admitting, "So he can shoot."

When Jim again reached Muga's side, the man quickly seized his gun back again.

The small hunting party, including Muga, set out very early the next morning. Jim noted the equipment which the men carried and also the happy, expectant look on their faces. The boy yearned for his home. He had seen just that look on his father's face whenever he headed into the woods.

Wapeuttequah worked the boy hard that day. The weather was getting colder and already there was a hint of snow in the air. The squaw was determined to get her harvest all stored for the winter before the snow started.

Jim watched the young braves play a different game that day. This time they kept yelling "*Shinny*" at one another. In this sport, which they played with curved sticks, the Indians used a leather ball. The aim seemed to be to hit the buckskin ball through a goal. The players ran as swiftly as horses. On the side of the field the small boys copied the young braves but used short sticks and a little block of wood for a ball. They screamed "*Shinny*" in their high, piercing voices and ran madly up and down. Occasionally the little ones became extremely angry and hit each other with their sticks.

The enjoyment that the young braves and boys were getting out of this made Jim Moore feel lonelier and more cut off than ever. Their shouts and gaiety cut him as no harsh words had. For these were human beings of his own age and they were having fun.

It was maddening to be owned by someone else. His father had never owned slaves. Of course, John Simpson had been an indentured servant when he had first come to them, but that was different. That just meant a man signed himself up to work for a length of time in return for certain things, such as his passage from England. The boy remembered the day his father had said, "Well, Simpson, you've earned your freedom. You've worked out your time. From now on you're as free as any other citizen of this new country and I'll pay you regular wages."

Jim choked back the ache in his heart. Just the thought of freedom hurt when there was so little chance of it. Deliberately he forced his thoughts toward hope. He murmured to himself as he walked along, "How do I know? Maybe the squaw might someday give me freedom if I serve her the way Simpson worked for Pa."

He kicked the dirt and went into the wigwam.

His owner was fearfully busy that night. In addition to fixing the herb brew for his feet, she cooked up a big kettle of hominy. The old woman's face occasionally burst into smiles and she moved with a new energy. Soon she squatted down and picked up some new moccasins she had been beading. She worked very fast and before long had them finished. Wapeuttequah appeared excited, as if she were preparing for some event.

Again the thought crossed the American lad's mind that the squaw might be working him harm with this nightly foot soaking. Still his feet had felt better since she started it. The sores that had formed on the stone bruises were healing up, and he could poke the stone bruises without pain. He decided that it couldn't be a trick, for the squaw liked having him do her work. No, she must really be trying to get him in good shape so he could do heavier work.

He studied Wapeuttequah's face. She was certainly planning something. He fell asleep trying to puzzle out what she might be up to.

It was bitterly cold the next morning when Jim felt the squaw shake him. Her red-brown face was filled with determination as she leaned over him. His first thought was, "She's going to kill me after all."

He quickly noticed that his owner was dressed in the same fine costume she had worn the night of his trial. She had pinned her collection of silver brooches on her soft deerskin blouse. In addition she wore all her necklaces. Jim had never seen so many before. Many of them were made of wampum beads but one was made of bear's teeth. So, the squaw's husband must have once been a fine hunter. His name meant "bear."

Jim knew from the amount of wampum Wapeuttequah wore and from her costume that he had been right in thinking her a rich Indian. That wampum was the same as money. Besides, hadn't she owned a horse, the one she had traded for him?

The squaw was in a hurry now. She pointed to the pot of hominy she had cooked the night before and then to Jim's mouth. Next the long bony finger indicated the kettle of herbs and the boy's feet. Immediately the majestic old woman stalked to the entrance and lifted the door flap. Standing with her arms spread across the door like a bar, she pointed to Jim, shook her head violently and made the motion of using a tomahawk on his head.

With that she disappeared from the wigwam.

Jim huddled back under the bearskin. He knew that the hominy was for him to eat, that he was to soak his feet and not to go out under penalty of death. What could this new turn of events mean?

Had his owner dressed up to go to a new council about him or had she gone somewhere to sell him? The boy wished now that the old warrior was back. He seemed quieter and more peaceful than the squaw.

Jim was too alarmed to go back to sleep but at least it was better to be under the furs than to get up, for the tiny fire the squaw had left did not begin to warm up the wigwam.

Finally he got so hungry that he crawled out of the skins and put some wood on the smoldering fire. For the hundredth time he wondered why Indians always kept such small fires when they had all of the forests available at their front door.

The boy heated up the lumpy white hominy. It filled his stomach and he felt better. Cautiously he tiptoed to the door flap and looked out. Just as he thought, a wizened old brave sat by a fire about twelve feet away. The old fellow had a gun across his knee.

So he *was* a prisoner, and he was being guarded. Jim cleaned up his bowl and sat by the fire awhile. Then he crawled back under the bearskins.

During the day the captive lad could hear the sounds of the nearby village and the going and coming of the women on their way to the spring. Every now and then the wind would waft happy, vigorous shouts from the playing field.

The young Virginian lay thinking about the Indians' love of games and sport. After a while he decided that this was the way the redskin people developed their bodies and kept in shape for war and long hunts. Nearly all the youths and men had splendidly developed bodies. Jim could see how football and shinny would build strong muscles and speed.

But then he remembered that he had often seen the old men playing a game on a big flat rock. So it wasn't just exercise they were after. They liked these games. That reminded him of a hired man his father had had at Abb's Valley one summer. The man had claimed to be Scottish and had always gone around whistling a tune called the "Highland Fling." This man had brought with him very few garments, but he did have a board marked off in designs and markers that he moved around on the board. John Simpson and Irish John had both played with the fellow, but his mother had not approved. He wondered why. While his father had never played, the other men seemed to enjoy the game. Maybe red men and white men were very much alike if they could only speak the same language. It was a thought he'd had before, and it kept popping back in his mind as he saw more of the way Indians lived.

But then across his memory flashed stories of scalping and brutal treatment along the frontier. He had always hated the tales of red men bashing in the heads of harmless infants. Yet after news of a raid, Jim remembered his father saying to his mother, "They're vicious and ruthless and I detest the thought of them, but remember they think we're stealing their hunting lands."

His father was like that, always trying to be fair. But few men on the frontier would have said such a thing. All they ever did was curse the "varmints."

The hours dragged by. It was dark in the wigwam and that added to the boy's loneliness. If only he had a book to read, it would help him to forget himself and the bad situation he was in. Since his capture, Jim had often thought with longing of the books on that shelf back in his home. There weren't many of them but, whenever he could, his father got more. That was one of the exciting things that happened when Captain Moore returned from selling horses. He usually managed to bring back at least one new book.

Lying under the bearskins here in this wigwam in the Ohio country, Jim thought of a boy he had known back on the Bluestone River not too many miles from his home. The boy couldn't read or write. There was no school anywhere in the area. Well, thank goodness his father had had a good education and had taught him. He hoped he wouldn't forget those things. But suddenly he had the appalling thought, "With nobody to talk to, you might forget how to speak English." That was crazy, his own speech was a part of him.

The boy felt as if he were dreaming. He could almost hear his mother correcting the way he spoke. "Now, son, take after your papa's nice talk. My brother Robert was brought up to speak nice but a blacksmith has to deal with some mighty rough folk and he just dropped into little slovenly ways of speech."

Once the lad pretended he was back in the valley with Prince Charlie. His colt was well trained and he was riding him. Oh, it was wonderful galloping over the bluegrass. A shout from a running Indian child outside the wigwam tore him out of his dream.

He got up to look out. Now there was a different old man on guard, but it was still an Indian brave holding a gun and plenty ready to use it.

Jim became convinced that Wapeuttequah was up to no good, wherever she was. That night he got down on his knees and prayed as he hadn't since he had left home. His mother and father had a real faith in God and they had taught their children to pray. Jim didn't say any fancy prayers. He just talked out loud to God and told Him all his troubles and how scared he was of being tortured if the Shawnees got angry and changed their minds about letting him live.

Jim felt better when he had finished. Afterward he even soaked his feet, deciding he wanted to be in good shape for whatever he might be facing.

The squaw did not return and Jim Moore was strongly tempted to try to escape that night. He peered out and saw someone still on guard by the fire. After watching a long time, Jim observed the man get up and move around. Worse luck, it was a young brave. So his owner had figured that he might try to get away under cover of night. She had put a fast young fellow on the job for the dangerous hours.

The boy sat in the wigwam counting up what chances he really had of getting clear away. Then he figured out all the things against it.

The chances of a successful escape were so slim that even Jim Moore, used to hardship on the frontier, had to admit to himself that it was worthless to try. He might make a fast dash and overpower that one guard, but how far could he get on the trail back home? How could he alone build a raft and propel it across the Ohio River? With the cold of winter having already set in, how could he live outdoors without a fire? If he lit a fire on his escape, he would soon be found by the Indians.

Up until this moment, the youthful Virginian had believed the time would come soon when he should make the effort to steal away. Now he made up his mind. He would have to spend at least the winter with the Shawnees and work toward a possible escape in the spring.

He decided that he would become as much one of the Shawnees as he could for the time he would be with them, learning all he could from and about them. He repeated frequently all the Indian words he had already learned and made a solemn promise to himself that he would work hard to learn to speak Shawnee, to hunt and trap like them, to know the woods and animal signs as they did. He resolved to toughen up his own body even more and to learn to do without food the way the red men could.

After these decisions were clear, the boy felt a sense

of hope coming back to him. He had a purpose now, a goal to work for. He would get himself ready to try for an escape when warm weather came again. He would not rely on someone else coming to rescue him, but he would plan how to do it himself.

8. Snake Belly's Hate

Jim Moore had been in solitary confinement for three days and three nights when his owner, the squaw Wapeuttequah, returned. She seemed very pleased with herself and showed the boy another silver brooch she had acquired. The woman was full of conversation and, from her words and gestures, Jim figured out she had been on a trip to another Indian village.

After she had talked herself out, the squaw examined Jim's feet. She appeared pleased at the improvement and actually smiled at him. In fact, Wapeuttequah acted so happy about everything that the young

American grew fearful that she had made a big bargain somewhere and sold him.

But in the days after that Wapeuttequah worked Jim hard, and before long she let him go out with the Indian boys to the nearby traps. The old squaw announced in the village that Shemanese was to have her husband's trapping rights. The first day she sent him out with a boy called Red Fox, whose shrewd eyes made him resemble the sly woods animal. Red Fox was very unwilling to take Jim along, but Wapeuttequah was his aunt and he had to do what she asked. By his attitude of contempt, Red Fox showed clearly that he didn't think Jim could catch anything. Only red men knew how to do that.

But Jim Moore had been setting traps for small animals since he was a young boy. He had started with a simple box trap for rabbits. He had a knack of placing them where they tempted the furry creatures. Now, he had a lucky break and caught several rabbits daily when some of the Indians did not catch anything.

Red Fox took the credit to himself as the Shawnee who had started Jim off. But one boy was furious over Jim's success. He came up very close to the Virginian and sneered, *"Shemanese weshe."*

The captive's face grew crimson. Now it was his turn to be furious. He would not let anyone call him "American dog." He grabbed the sneering Indian and tried to hurl him to the ground. The redskin, who was called Snake Belly, was not as tall as Jim, but he was wiry and strong and as slippery as an eel. He twisted and turned and prevented Jim from getting a really good hold on him. Then he wiggled his body upward like an augur worm and seized the American's head in a viselike grip. He started forcing it backward but Jim fought hard. Jim hooked his foot around Snake Belly's ankle and thus tossed them both to earth. The two rolled and twisted, writhed and slithered like snakes. It was a vicious contest to see who could stand it the longest. All the young Shawnees had gathered around and were yelling.

Jim had not yet recovered his full strength after the arduous trip from Virginia and the changeover to Indian food and the rather slim portions he had been fed. At one point in the struggle the boy felt panicky for fear he would not have the power to overcome this slippery redskin.

Then he caught a glimpse of all the young braves watching them and he knew it was now or never. If he failed in this test of strength, no Shawnee would ever have any use for him. He sucked in a very deep breath and with a mighty heave broke the Indian's lock on his head. Then pulling up a hidden reserve of strength from deep down inside, the Virginia boy rolled out from under his Indian adversary and pulled himself up on his knees. The Indian reared up to grab him but Jim leaped forward and pinned Snake Belly's shoulders flat to the ground.

The Shawnee grunted and heaved and did everything he could to throw Jim off, but the American boy was fighting for more than just to win a wrestling contest. He could not be budged.

After a minute or two of this continuing struggle the crowd shouted, "Ai, ai," and Young Wolf and another Indian came over to signal Jim to rise as the victor.

From that time on Jim had the respect of most of the young Indians. They soon admitted him to their games. His feet were still too tender to kick the football very well. But at shinny he proved a fast player. However, they were extremely skilled and Jim merely managed to hold his own with the Shawnee youths.

At first, Wapeuttequah was violently opposed to her slave playing in the games. But one of the warriors spoke to her and changed her mind. The American lad was eaten up with curiosity over what the brave had said. But he suspected that the warrior had told the squaw that she should not want a boy around who was not strong and healthy.

One thing that astonished the Virginia lad was the Indians' love of children. He could not get over how much they enjoyed the youngsters. He often saw grownups taking time to fashion toys for the little ones. It didn't make sense that people like this could go to white men's cabins and scalp their children. He puzzled over this, for he had thought that the redskins would be vicious all the way through and act haughty and cruel to small ones.

The tall American boy had all he could do to hold back tears the first time he saw the small bronze-red children play "treading the beaver." It reminded him so much of his little brothers and sisters back home and their favorite game, "blind man's bluff."

But the fact that amazed Jim beyond anything else was finding out that Indians were just as fond of dogs as his own family. There were many puppies in the village where he was captive. A number of the girls dressed the puppies like papooses and hung them over their backs in slings. The older people chuckled over this make-believe and enjoyed the fun.

One day a little boy let Jim try out a game he had. It was a sharp pointed stick and a pumpkin ring tied to it by a piece of vine. Jim took it to try to catch the ring on the stick as skillfully as the child, Little Otter, had done it.

Just at that moment his owner, Wapeuttequah, came looking for him and waved imperiously for him to come back with her at once. There was nothing for Jim to do except go. But, as he turned to leave, Little Otter handed him the toss game and smiled. The boy said very quietly so only Jim could hear it the name they all used for him, "Shemanese."

It was the only time anyone had spoken the word "American" in that kind way. It made him feel all warm inside. This was the first happy moment he had had since he left Abb's Valley.

Jim had made a friend but he had also made an enemy, the Indian youth, Snake Belly. From the moment the American had beaten him at wrestling, the lithe young redskin had begun to work against him. Each day Snake Belly had tried to keep Jim from the games. Not succeeding at that, the bitter youth quickly tried a new tactic. He observed that Jim was careful about his feet because they were still tender. In shinny games, whenever the chance came, he cracked the American's feet with his shinny stick.

One afternoon, in a football game, Jim was playing on the same side as Snake Belly. The yellow-haired boy had a great chance for a kick through the goal posts but missed. Snake Belly made a great scene,

laughing uproariously at Jim. He pointed contemptu-
ously to the white lad's feet and made him lift them
up. There was still one unhealed place and scars of
others. Snake Belly's two special friends joined him in
pushing Jim off the field.

The boy had noticed Little Otter and some of his
friends watching the game from the sidelines. When
Jim walked away from the field, the small boy came
over and joined him. When they reached Wapeuttequah's wigwam, Little Otter babbled out to the squaw
what had happened. The proud old Wapeuttequah
was very angry. Had not her own half-brother Black
Wolf captured this boy and had she not given a horse
for him? Nothing that belonged to her should be badly
treated in her village. She would take steps.

With his handful of words, Jim did his best to persuade her not to say anything about Snake Belly, declaring, "Shemanese take care of himself."

And so a struggle began that was to last a long time.
Snake Belly was not the only Shawnee who did not like
the American boy. Little Otter told him there were
some old women who said keeping him there was dangerous to the village. But these old crones never took
steps against him. Snake Belly, however, never missed
a chance to work a trick against Jim Moore. He even
stooped so low as to steal small game out of Jim's traps
and then go around announcing that Shemanese couldn't
even provide for an old squaw.

The hunting party now returned. Wapeuttequah's
husband was disgusted. He had never seen game so
scarce. The party had had very bad luck. He himself
had managed to shoot two deer but some of the men

had gotten only small animals. They had not killed a single bear. The braves sat around the fires muttering, and over and over Jim heard the words, "White men kill too much."

As the young Virginian came to understand more of the Shawnee language he could better understand the tales that were unfolded at night by the fires. There were stories of a bad man they did not like in Pennsylvania and also talk about Daniel Boone. One Indian who had traveled down into the Kentucky area said, "Him red man enemy. He kill and kill. He no hungry, no need so much meat. Him just kill take home skins. Leave no hunting for Indian. No animals, then no meat. No meat, then Indian hungry. Kentucky Indians' land. No white men should come."

That man's words stuck in the minds of the young Shawnees. They talked about it and wondered when the whole tribe would do something about trouble the white men gave. Also, Black Wolf was back in the village now, and wherever he was there was always growling talk against the white settlers. The tall minor chief with the black beard said over and over, "White men steal our land."

Jim noticed that, while the young braves never failed to agree with Black Wolf's warlike talk, the old chieftain of the village looked worried and said little.

The people of the village had looked forward to the meat and skins that the hunters, including Wapeut-tequah's husband, would bring in. Now, with the poor results, there was a gloom over the village. Some of the old crones said that food had been scarce enough the year before, they would hate to see it any worse. Several ancient braves declared that the winter ahead would be severe. The medicine man disappeared into his wigwam, worked magic for several days, and reappeared to confirm this statement. He predicted there would be much cold and snow.

The head chief checked on how much food there was on hand for the winter. The braves did little but huddle around fires, muttering among themselves.

One morning Jim noticed that Black Wolf had freshly shaved the hair off half his head and looked just the way he did when he appeared in Abb's Valley.

Something was going on among the men that the captive could not make out. The braves were all acting very mysterious. During one whole day Jim noticed the senior men of the village giving a signal to each other whenever they thought they weren't observed. It was something they did with their fingers and after that they would say very solemnly, "*Powwow.*"

That afternoon Wapeuttequah cooked only venison, the meat of the deer her husband had brought home. After he had eaten, the old warrior dressed in his finest clothes and wrapped himself in his mantle of matched skins. He stood before the door flap and very solemnly intoned the word, "*Powwow,*" and left the wigwam.

Jim Moore was choking with curiosity but the old squaw paid no attention to him. She only gazed in the fire and said solemnly, "*Wysheana Powwow.*"

The boy knew no more than before because all she had said was, "My husband, Powwow."

But the next morning Jim was able to find out a bit from Little Otter. At first the Indian boy only rolled his eyes and acted mysterious, but Jim kept on teasing to find out. Finally Little Otter whispered, "Powwow brotherhood of brave men. Only good ones. Big meeting last night."

Throughout that day the men still looked solemn but they stayed busy. Jim knew the signs because it was just like back home. The men were certainly getting ready for a big hunt.

Wapeuttequah was busy curing the skins of the deer her husband had brought. Jim had to keep a slow smudge fire and keep turning the skins toward the smoke. Then they jerked all the meat that was left by smoking it over the fire.

The braves were more excited now than the American had ever seen them. They cleaned their guns and sharpened axes. The squaws stretched blankets out in the pale midday sun to air them for the long trip.

Jim was next assigned to haul wood to a big wigwam they called the sweat house. A great fire was kept going there and rocks heated in it. The heat in the place seemed unendurable to Jim whenever he had to go in. Gradually all the braves going on the long hunt went to the sweat house. Some spent four days there. Little Otter explained to Jim, "Braves sweat hard. Get very wet. Makes men strong."

Jim noticed that the process also made them much leaner, for in the sweat house they ate no food but drank a tea made from bitter roots.

There was no talk in the village these days of anything else but the hunt. Black Wolf was to go, and he boasted of all the game he would kill. He would come back rich with skins to trade to white men. He would bring much meat for the village. In his arrogant way he pointed to the exploit feathers that jutted out from his little skullcap.

Jim Moore felt sick over this big hunting party going out and leaving only the old warriors, women and children in the village. He would be left behind to do woman's work just like one of the squaws. More than ever he felt his position as a captive slave. He didn't even have the heart to talk to Little Otter.

That night Wapeuttequah was busy making leggings out of the newly cured skins. She tried them on Jim's legs. Up until now he had had only the old cast-off moccasins of Wapeuttequah's. His legs were still bare.

The next day the squaw sewed steadily. She measured Jim's feet and worked on a new pair of moccasins. But she still kept her mouth shut and would tell him nothing.

As Jim staggered into the sweat house with a big load of wood, Black Wolf ordered him to bring no more but to take off his clothes and sit down and sweat with the other young men.

Jim's heart pounded with excitement. This must mean he was to go with them on the hunt. Young Wolf, the chief's son, was in the sweat house and saw the excitement of the boy who had dragged him back on the raft on the Ohio. He nodded his head up and down.

That night Wapeuttequah worked late. She had Jim fill two skin pouches of parched corn and she herself laid out jerked meat, powder and shot, and her husband's gun. She gave the boy the new moccasins and leggings and some buckskin with which to patch any tears he made in his clothing.

9. Black Wolf's Hunt

It was early the next morning when the hunters set out through the woods, and that night the first snow fell. Black Wolf shook his head and muttered, "Old men right. Hard winter coming. Snow heavy soon."

And hard it was. The weather grew steadily colder and the snow never let up.

For days the party saw nothing but small game. They ate the fresh meat and kept only the pelts. On they marched, swinging in a great circle to the north.

Black Wolf was a stern leader. Each morning, as light began to streak the sky, the black-bearded leader would have the youths bring in great quantities of wood. He personally heaped them on the fire. Then he would stand and yell a command, *"Thebowithe,"* if they were camped by a small stream, or *"Sepe"* if they were near a river. The young Shawnees, pretending they didn't mind, would yell "Ai, ai" and dash down to the water, break the ice and jump in. They bathed rapidly in the cruel cold, all the time shouting and splashing to show how hardy and brave they were.

The first morning on the trail, when Black Wolf had ordered the youths into the water, Jim had noticed Snake Belly trying to avoid going. The lithe young Indian had pretended that there was not enough wood for the fire and had kept on bringing it in. That first time when Jim had hit the icy stream he had thought his heart would just stop beating, but he was determined to die rather than act like Snake Belly. Somehow the Virginian lived through the ordeal and ran back up the bank shouting with the Shawnees.

To Jim's delight, at that moment Black Wolf discovered Snake Belly and pushed him into the water. While the Indians laughed at the event, the American looked the other way and never cracked a smile. He had had enough trouble with Snake Belly without stirring up any more.

Each morning when the youths emerged from the icy waters, Black Wolf shouted a second command which was gladly obeyed. His order *"Scoote!"* sent them racing for the big fire. There they dried themselves by the heat of the flames, put on their clothes made of animal skins, and leaped around the fire to get invigorated for the day. They cracked their parched

corn on a rock and tossed it into a kettle of boiling water. At this time of day there was always hope that in
the hours ahead they would meet up with big game and
make a mighty killing.

With the frugal morning meal inside them, the
hunters would then be divided into small groups to
fan out in opposite directions. One day Jim found
tracks that he was sure had been made by a bear. He
tracked further and further into the woods, away from
his party until behind a thicket, up ahead, he saw a
great black form. The young American quickly took
aim and had the bead right on the animal. Suddenly
he felt a jostle of his arm and his gun went off. The
great black hulk of bear tore off. Jim tried to reload
and shoot but it was too late. The animal had gotten
away. Who had sneaked up from behind on him like
that and pulled such a dirty trick? He knew before he
swiveled around and faced Snake Belly.

The other hunters in their group joined them now
and all that day they trailed the bear but never over-
took him. That night around the campfire, Snake Belly
regaled the entire hunting party with his own version
of how Jim had missed aim on the bear. There was
nothing Jim could say. His word would not be taken
against a full-blooded Shawnee. Snake Belly laughed
mockingly and announced, "Bad medicine to bring
white slave. White boy no good. He cause evil spirit.
Evil spirit go ahead of us and chase animals away, we
no shoot game."

To miss a bear was serious, doubly serious since the
big hairy animals would all soon be in hibernation.
Snake Belly made constant references to Jim's failure

and kept it fresh in the minds of the other hunters. Jim received much unfriendly treatment after this episode.

The boy was determined to redeem himself before the other Shawnees. But there was little game and therefore little chance.

In his sleep, Jim dreamed always of the meals his mother cooked back home. When awake, he would often recall that last supper he had had in Abb's Valley, the chicken and the huckleberry pudding.

The boy was constantly hungry, and at night he was miserable from cold as well. The one blanket Wapeut-tequah had given him was too short for his long body. He curled himself up like a snail to try to keep covered. But every morning his legs and spine were so cramped he could hardly move.

Black Wolf would order camp set up in one spot for several days at a time and they worked out from there. This permitted them to build crude shelters of pine boughs which at least kept the snow from covering them at night.

The hunt dragged on and on. If they had been finding game, Jim would have enjoyed it in spite of his hunger, the cold and the tricks Snake Belly was constantly trying on him. It was hard, too, to camp night after night and hear his companions blame the lack of game on the white man.

Late one afternoon Jim finally sighted a fine buck of a deer. The majestic horns on the animal were projecting beyond a bush. Jim inched slowly around to where he could get a good aim. He had to steady his arm, for his great eagerness made him tremble. This time there was no Snake Belly and the shot brought down the handsome buck. Black Wolf decreed that each of the hunters could have a small piece of venison, but the rest had to be smoked to be taken back to the village.

The frontier boy, when he lay down for the night, carefully noted their position by the stars. In January they started moving southward. By the end of the month they were nearing the home village in the Scioto River country.

Runners were sent out to advise of the approaching return of the hunters. A half day's journey from the village, a group of old warriors, squaws and youngsters met the long-absent party. Great was the disappointment of all about the quantity of meat and small number of skins the group had brought back.

Black Wolf gathered the village inhabitants around him and made a speech denouncing the white men for having killed so much game. "You say 'Hunters no good.' Braves who went through snow tell you no animals there. If brave not find animal, cannot kill. White men been before. Killed all."

Jim thought it was as good a way as any for Black Wolf to make people forget all the boasting he had done before they left.

In the remaining winter months, the captive lad hunted out from the home village. No long hunt was again attempted, even though food supplies were very low. It was decided that such a big effort was not worth what they would get.

The Shawnees were none too happy in those late

winter months. The men felt the lack of meat in the cook pots was a reflection on their skill and their bad humor made them cross or silent in the wigwams. This general bad temper took real hold on Snake Belly. One day Jim found the tricky redskin lurking at the rear of Wapeuttequah's wigwam. There was a broken place in one of the woven mats that formed the wall structure. The Virginian noticed that Snake Belly had a sharp tool in his hand. Jim looked very pointedly from the tool to the hole. Snake Belly looked a trifle uneasy but quickly said, "Shemanese such bad shot. Snake Belly never forget day Shemanese missed bear. Ha-ha-ha."

With that, the slinky Indian walked away.

Just inside the wall through which Snake Belly had been boring was a pile of Wapeuttequah's treasured belongings. Jim guessed that the Indian would have stolen the things and blamed it on him. That was the narrowest escape the boy had had from the constant trickery of the Shawnee who so hated him.

One day in the woods Jim discovered a small cave where squirrels had hidden quantities of nuts, both chestnuts and black walnuts. The furry ones had eaten about half their winter supply. Jim felt like a thief as he carried off the rest.

He took his rich loot to the squaw who owned him but not until after he had hidden some to give to Little Otter.

On one very bitter day, Wapeuttequah's husband had to remain under the bearskins. The squaw had no one with whom to play her endless game on the flat stone, so she taught Jim to play. The boy found this more amusing than having nothing to do. It kept him from thinking about home, his family and his colt.

Muga continued so stiff with rheumatism that he seldom left the wigwam fire. Jim often pondered how Wapeuttequah and her husband could have lived through the winter without the food he brought in. When there was no game Jim fished through a hole in the ice on a nearby pond. It meant long freezing hours before he got a bite and, sometimes the fish weren't more than a mouthful.

When there were any animals in the woods Jim got his share. The Indians openly admired his skill in trapping. That is, all except Snake Belly, who kept up his enmity.

Jim came to realize how hard life was for these people of the forest, certainly for the old ones. Back on the Virginia frontier, difficult as things were there, the poorest settlers had more food and warmth than this old squaw even though she owned those two piles of valuable possessions.

These were grim days in the Shawnee village. The only person who had a smile for Jim was Little Otter. The small boy was terribly thin but tried to be a good sport.

Finally one piece of good luck came Jim's way. Young Wolf, son of the chief, and a brave named Big Rib asked Jim if he would go on a three-day hunt with them. Jim got only a few squirrels but Young Wolf brought down a moose. It was a huge animal and meant excellent eating for the village for a while at least. When the three arrived back in the settlement, even Jim was praised.

As soon as they had received the acclaim of the hungry people, Young Wolf started running through the village yelling, "Snow snake."

The presiding chief smiled and said, "Good. My people need celebration."

Big Rib gave Young Wolf a signal and together they picked up a chunky little boy who was standing near. The youngster was wrapped in a grimy blanket as protection against the cold. Even as they carried him off to the playing field the boy was happily screeching, "Snow snake."

Once at the field the braves dragged the chunky little boy back and forth on the snow to pack down a lane for the "snake" to travel. The little boy's cheeks got redder than ever but he didn't seem to mind.

From every wigwam came streaming the young braves and youths of the village. Each one carried smooth sticks which had been rubbed with tallow.

The old warriors were telling the women how to build a huge fire right by the side of the playing area. Now the youths formed into teams, Young Wolf heading one and Big Rib the other. The teams went to the two different ends of the snow lane.

Jim quickly saw why the sport was called "snow snake." The players had a knack of hurling the smoothly polished sticks so that they wriggled and skittered down the snowy lane. The American watched the way they threw the sticks. There was a twist to it but mostly, he figured, the snaking motion was caused by the heavy heads on the sticks.

The players were slipping and sliding too much as they made their tosses. Young Wolf called to Jim to get ashes and spread them at the head of each lane. Little Otter followed Jim away from the playing field and asked if he could help.

The youthful teams played a long time and then some of the older men drew up sides and had a go at it. The game required skill so naturally there was never any chance for Jim to get in on it since he'd never seen it played before.

That evening, after the entertaining sport, pieces of the moose meat were given to each family. The smell of roasting meat could be sniffed throughout the village.

Everyone was well fed and happy. Temporarily, at least, they could forget their hardships. The presiding chief decided his people needed to continue the celebration. He had all four fires in the council house heaped up with wood and asked the people in. Various elderly men told tales of the Shawnees, how they had once lived by a water with salt in it, how they had moved once and moved again, always north. They spoke of the time their people had dwelled in Pennsylvania and why they had gone over into the Ohio country where they lived now. Tales of bravery were recounted by some of the braves.

Jim Moore was surprised by how much he understood. He did not know some words that the speakers used but he could get the meaning from the gesticulations.

Finally some of the women called out, "Tell us of the magical serpent." And this ancient story, told by the medicine man, went on and on.

Jim was barely able to keep his eyes open when at

last, in a rising voice, the medicine man ended his
speech by calling on the Great Spirit to dwell among
the Shawnees that they might be brave.

It was an exciting evening to cap a fine afternoon.
But it was the last Jim was to have for some months.
The days dragged along and the skies stayed gray and
sullen. Jim knew that by this time his home valley in
Virginia would be showing signs of spring. But not
here. He thought that the snow would never melt and
go away.

Gradually a few more animals stirred abroad in the
woods. The near-starvation diet of the village was im-
proved but Jim still felt hungry most of the time. At
last in April there was warmth in the air and the captive boy began to think again of escape.

He had hoped that by now he would have found one
Indian friendly enough to him to give him a little help
on the first part of the flight. But, while most of the
village people had accepted him, there was no evidence
that a single one would help a captive to escape. Not
even Little Otter; he was too great a believer in the
code of the Shawnees.

Many of the youths with whom Jim had played
games had been going through their preparation to become braves. These boys, between fifteen and seventeen, had finished their stern training. All winter they
had been looking forward to spring as the time for
their initiation into the full stature of manhood. The
ceremony was a great event. Jim was amazed at what
emphasis they put on their first pipe. This was an important ritual and a very solemn one. They used real

tobacco, which by this time was very scarce. Jim had heard that soon, if no traders came, some braves would go to the white settlements to trade pelts for tobacco. After the ceremony, the new braves strutted around the village as if they were kings. The young girls made a huge fuss over them.

One day the old braves again went around the village quietly giving a signal with their fingers and murmuring, "*Powwow.*"

Now that Jim understood Shawnee he found out more about the Powwow Club or Brotherhood. He learned that membership in the society was considered a great honor and that the meetings were of a very solemn nature. The meeting this spring was to be in a nearby village, Wapotomatick.

Wapeuttequah's husband was at last able to move around again now that the weather was warmer. His rheumatism was still painful, but he was not as stiff as he had been. On the day set for the Powwow meeting, the old warrior once more dressed in his finery and set off with a solemn face for the secret conclave.

Two days later Wapeuttequah saw her husband returning. She went out to meet him but he barely spoke and marched straight into the wigwam and crouched down by the fire. He sat there gazing into the flames, speaking not at all.

Jim thought the old man's face was sadder than anything he had ever seen before. The boy straightened out the skins on the sleeping platform and pretended not to notice how worried the squaw was. She kept peering at her husband yet trying to act as if she were

not doing so. Finally she could stand his strange behavior no longer. She went in front of him and kneeled
down.

Wapeuttequah's voice was humble and scared. Jim
was startled by the tone in it as she said, "*Wysheana,*
my husband, tell me, what is wrong? Why are you so
sad?"

The old warrior continued to look miserable and did
not answer. But the squaw repeated the question. She
urged him in many ways.

Finally he said, "During our meeting a spirit proceeded out of the medicine the medicine man had
made. The spirit appeared to us. At first we saw nothing larger than a man's hand."

The sad-looking man held out his own hand and
stared at it. With an effort he resumed, "Then it got
larger and larger until it was the size of a boy twelve
years old." The old warrior raised his hand to the height
of a boy.

"The spirit was very angry with us people of the
Shawnee. The spirit recounted all the good deeds of
our ancestors. Then it spoke sadly of our bad deeds of
today. The spirit said we have left the way of our fathers and become proud and lazy and forsaken broth-
erly love. Spirit say 'In olden day, paths of Shawnee
marked with track of men and dogs, but now only with
the track of horses.' "

The old warrior stared at his wife and at Jim Moore
and repeated the word "horses." The boy supposed the
man was reminding her that she had bought a boy with
a horse. Also Jim knew that whenever her half-brother

Black Wolf came to the wigwam, the two sat and talked about the horses they were going to get hold of one way or another. Jim thought more than ever then about Prince Charlie and the other horses back home in Abb's Valley.

The squaw's husband continued now, "The spirit said Shawnees used to give to brother who came naked and destitute. But now a brother must pay or go away without food or clothing."

The voice sank lower and lower and got even sadder. "The Great Spirit is going to chastise us for our wickedness and the villages, Wapatomatick, Major Jack and Kismagogee, are all to be destroyed."

Then, pointing to the squaw's embroidered hangings, to two silver brooches that Wapeuttequah was wearing and to the pile of belongings that she kept in the wigwam, the old warrior suddenly said very sternly, "And you, Wapeuttequah, will be punished for your pride."

Jim could not bear to look at his owner after he saw the first look of hurt come over her face. She was stunned into silence. The boy knew that, according to her idea, she had been a good wife.

The captive stole silently out of the wigwam. He could not stand to hear any more.

Jim stayed out of doors as much as he could after that night, for there was now great strain and sadness between his owner and her husband. The boy built more traps; he went hunting whenever Young Wolf or Big Rib wanted him to. When he wasn't hunting he was fishing in the streams that were not clear of ice.

10. A Festival and a Sale

As the sap rose higher in the trees and the women got the tools ready for the spring planting, the time arrived for the spring festival. The great dance was to be held at the village called Major Jack, two miles from where Jim's owner lived. This name had often fascinated Jim. He wondered if some white man by that name had once been captured by the people of that village.

The winter had lasted so long and been so hard that everyone in the village was particularly excited over the festival. Jim was as anxious to go as any of the Shawnees. He felt he would burst if something exciting didn't happen soon. But the old warrior and Wapeutte-quah seemed as sad as could be. He began to fear that they would not go and that therefore he would not be able to go. No word of the festival was ever mentioned in the wigwam.

All over the village there were stirrings of people getting ready for the colorful event. Early on the morning it was to begin, families began to take the trail for the village of Major Jack.

Muga shook his head gloomily and went off into the woods as if he could not stand the sight of so much gaiety. Immediately, Wapeuttequah dressed herself in her finest clothes and pinned silver brooches all over her blouse. Taking Jim with her, she set off for the festival.

The dancing had begun when the two arrived. The celebration was being held on the field where the village men usually played their games. Two great circles of Shawnees had formed. One was of men, the other of women. The American boy was astonished to see so many people.

The men were dancing in strong powerful movements. They were chanting one of their songs of friendship. The opening words were, "A friend you resemble," but by the second verse the warriors were singing, "Brothers I think we are."

Jim saw some of the girls who had recently had their fifteenth birthday and completed the ceremony for becoming a woman. They looked particularly happy in a

dance they and the others did about the spring planting.

To his amazement, when the dance ended, he
glanced across the field to see Wapeuttequah talking
to a white man. The boy shaded his eyes against the
sun to be sure. Yes, it really was a white man—the first
he had seen since his capture. Immediately a dozen
ideas rushed into his mind. Would this white man
maybe help him to escape? Had the man come from the
Virginia settlements after him? Or had he at least
brought a message from his people? Then the awful
thought occurred to him that maybe Wapeuttequah was
bargaining with the man to sell him.

The man had two huge bags and was emptying one of
them before his owner. He knew how Wapeuttequah
loved to trade. This did not look good. If he had to be
owned by anyone he certainly did not want to be sold
away from the village where Little Otter lived. The boy
was his friend and Wapeuttequah was not unkind.

He must see what he could do. He ran around the
field to the side of his owner. The man was kneeling
down, displaying a collection of glittering glass beads
and silver pins. He had already spread out some bright
ribbons and a large batch of tin pans. Wapeuttequah
was talking rapidly and Jim could not break in.

It seemed so strange to see a white man again. His
hair was very black and he seemed rather swarthy of
skin. Maybe being out on the trail with his pack made
him look different from the people back in Virginia.
The boy could hardly wait to talk to the man. Finally
he tugged at Wapeuttequah's sleeve. She stopped talking and the man looked up. Jim immediately burst out

with the question of whether he had come from the Virginia settlements.

The trader's face looked blank. He replied with a volley of fast words that he spit out of his mouth in a nervous sort of way.

Jim's great hopes sank to his toes. The man was not an American, not even British from Canada. The peddler was still talking and waving his hands. Jim decided he must be French.

Springing up, the man put both hands on Jim's shoulders and gave him a big smile. He said, "Me, Baptiste Ariome."

The boy was amused by the accent and replied, "Me, James Moore, called Jim."

The Frenchman was delighted and answered right back, "Hallo, Jim, you handsome boy."

Jim Moore's face turned scarlet. He was not used to compliments.

Wapeuttequah was too interested in the goods the trader had spread out to pay any attention to the two.

Mr. Ariome walked around Jim in a circle, looking at him. The boy felt humiliated. This was the first time a white man had ever studied him as if he were a horse. This was just the way his father and Simpson sized up an animal back home.

But the Frenchman kept smiling at him and finally said, *Cher garçon*, you so like my son. He dead two months—my oldest son. You forgive if I look at you."

There was a dance around the campfire that night. Twice Mr. Ariome came up to talk to Jim. The boy asked him if he ever traded as far as Virginia. "*Non*, me stick to Pen-seel-vania, Oheeo and Nieu York, big

enough for Baptiste." He laughed gaily at his own remark.

Jim was crushed. Even after finding out the man was
French, he had hoped maybe he traded down south too
and would take a message to the Moores. But Ariome
made it clear he would have no way even to send a message. Jim realized the man was too anxious to trade
with the Shawnees to risk in any way helping a captive
to escape or seek rescue.

The festival continued the next day. The dancing
was even more exciting on the second day. But Jim noticed that his owner was not watching the performance.
She was off to the side talking with Mr. Ariome. He
saw her, out of the corner of his eye, as she fondled
silver brooches that the trader had brought. Well, why
should he worry just because the old squaw wanted to
acquire more jewelry? Muga would be angry when
they returned, but that wasn't the worst thing in the
world.

The boy turned to watch a dance by the young
women. At that moment he felt a hand clapped on
his shoulder. Jim whirled around to face Mr. Ariome.

The French trader was one large smile. "You now be
my boy, just like my son. I trade squaw-woman fifty
dollairs' worth of goods for you."

Jim Moore was stunned. He had become used to his
life among the Shawnees. Now that it was getting
warm, his hopes had risen that he would find a way to
escape from the Indians and return to Virginia down
the route he knew. Every night during his long captivity the boy had gone over in his mind exactly how
Black Wolf had come north. The Virginia boy be-

lieved that, if he could just get across the Ohio River, he could find his way back to Abb's Valley, far though it was. But now, just when things looked hopeful, here was this man saying he had bought him.

The boy blurted out fiercely, "Where do you come from, where do you live?"

Ariome looked hurt. "Why in *la belle* Canada, of course. Across from Detroit." The trader pronounced the words in a strange way.

Jim felt as though the bottom of his world had fallen out. He would be leaving people who had been fairly decent to him. But worst of all, he would be going farther and farther from home. Once away up in Canada, what chance would he have to escape?

The lad tried to figure out some way he could escape that very day. But there were so many people around. Once the boy started off toward the woods to see what would happen. He had not gone a hundred feet before a little girl came running after him to say Wapeutte-quah wanted him to bring her a drink of water. So he knew that the squaw was keeping an eagle eye on him. He was about to make one final effort to sneak away when he overheard two braves talking about how swollen the Ohio was. One said it was too rough for a raft right now. So that shattered Jim's dream.

However, he never stopped puzzling over what he should try to do. One thing he knew was that he wanted to see Little Otter before he was taken away. It took him some time to locate the friendly little boy. He was at the opposite end of the playing field looking at shiny baubles displayed by another trader. It was not Ariome. Jim almost danced a jig when he heard the trader speak English words. And the man spoke them with the peculiar twist of the American frontiersman. This was language Jim Moore understood.

In a rush of words, he introduced himself.

The trader looked at him with curiosity and said, "My name's Sherlock. Used to be a prisoner here with these Injuns myself."

Jim wanted to give the man a big bear hug. He literally hurled questions at the trader. Little Otter could not understand a word of what they were saying, but he saw how happy Jim was to be talking to the man.

Finally Mr. Sherlock said, "I'll forget me sales for a piece and set over here on this log. I reckon 'twould be best if you told me yer whole dang tale."

The burly trader listened with the keenest interest and occasionally grunted encouragement to Jim to go on with the story. He punctuated everything by spitting out the juice of the tobacco he was chewing. When Jim finished and asked if there wasn't some way Sherlock could help him to escape, the trader shook his head in sorrow.

"Tarnation, son, you're lucky to still have that yellow head o' hair on you. 'Taint a thing I can do to spirit you out of here. It's thisaway. Once I managed to save a boy named Moffatt. The Injuns had captured him down to the headwaters of the Clinch River. Ever since, the redskins watch me close."

Jim shouted at the man, "Did Moffatt's father move to Kentucky?"

It was now the turn of the trader to be surprised. He said, "Yeah, he sure did, but how come you know that?"

"Mr. Moffatt is a friend of my pa's. Mr. Sherlock, you've just got to get word to him about me. If you'd only pass the word to him, I know he would manage to get it back to my home."

Sherlock grunted. He kept twisting his mouth and finally said, "I knows how violent you feels. Just like being hawg-tied, ain't it? Just terrible being a prisoner. What you want me to do?"

"Write a letter or get one written and send it to Mr. Moffatt. Tell him what I just told you but tell him that my Shawnee owners just sold me to a French trader named Baptiste Ariome. Say that Mr. Ariome's taking me to his home near Detroit but over in Canada."

Sherlock let out a whistle. "Ye saved that bit, Moore. You hadn't told me they traded you. Well, I cross paths with Baptiste some places. He ain't a bad feller. The French ain't as funny as most folks think they is."

Jim wondered what he could give Mr. Sherlock so that he would take the trouble to send the letter. He took off two beaded wrist bands he had made himself. He handed them to the trader.

Little Otter, who all this time had been crouching nearby on the ground looking at the trader's goods, saw what Jim had done. He quickly took off a shell he wore hung around his neck, handed it to Mr. Sherlock and nodded toward Jim.

The man whistled. Then he looked at Little Otter and back at Jim. He chuckled, "So, there's one Injun that likes you even if he is just a tadpole."

At this moment Wapeuttequah came up. She was cross because she had been looking for Jim everywhere. She ordered him to come with her right away

and marched him around the field to where Mr. Ariome was waiting. The trader from Canada had handed
over one whole pack of goods to the Indian squaw in return for Jim. The other he had sold or traded to others.
His packs being empty, he was anxious to start home-
ward. The bags did not long stay empty, however, for
the Frenchman was busy stuffing them with the furs and
skins which he had secured from the Shawnees at the
festival.

Wapeuttequah gave Jim the blanket he had used the
night before, sleeping out on the meadow, along with
the young braves gathered for the dance. She also
handed him a new pair of moccasins. The boy guessed
that she had brought these to trade but had decided to
give them to him instead. The old squaw's face had a
funny look on it. She patted Jim on his head and turned
swiftly and walked away.

Little Otter had followed them and stood nearby.
He was trying to be brave but his mouth quivered.

There was nothing Jim could think of to say. Finally
he blurted out, "You are my friend. I will never forget. Sometime maybe I can come back to see you if I
am ever free man."

Little Otter said, "If Great Spirit wish it, you come
back. You braver than any brave."

Those words helped to make the hurt less for Jim as
he trudged northward with his new owner.

Baptiste Ariome loved to talk. Jim soon found this
out on the trip to Canada. The trader's combination of
French and broken English was hard for the Virginia
boy to understand. The Frenchman spoke often of the

son he had lost and each time tears came to his eyes.

One morning, as they were swinging along a well-beaten Indian path, the Frenchman turned and said, "Jim, you make story of your life for me very quick now. Then, poof, we blow it to ze wind and it is gone. We forget it, yes? After that, you be Baptiste Ariome's boy, just like son that is gone. All mine."

Jim told his story, but he knew that he could not forget his past life and his own people.

When they reached the Ariome home in Canada, Jim felt as if he were at the other end of the world from his family. It seemed crazy to him but he suddenly missed the Shawnees. However, the young members of the Ariome family were anxious to make friends and would not leave him alone to mope. A daughter, Clarisse, was very nearly Jim's own age while Pierre, the remaining son, was a year younger. Then there was a very small girl named Marie.

It felt strange to him to be in a house again. His first night he just couldn't sleep. He was sharing Pierre's little room and kept him awake. Jim could not get comfortable on the soft feather mattress. He longed for the hard platform in Wapeuttequah's wigwam. Finally he got up, wrapped himself in the blanket the old squaw had given him and slept on the floor.

At breakfast Mrs. Ariome said, "It is miracle that Indians did not kill you. We happy to have you as son. *Le bon Dieu,* He is good."

Jim knew he ought to feel that way too, for the Ariomes did not treat him as a slave. They had him eat with them and gave him the same food they themselves had. They expected him to work hard, but his father had taught him how to plow and plant and the farm work helped to make the days pass.

The summer was nearly over and the vegetables gathered and stored when one evening Mr. Ariome asked his wife, "How soon before calf she is ready to be sold?"

Mrs. Ariome held up one finger. "You wait one more week. Calf then bring much more money."

At the end of that time, Papa Baptiste took the calf, some wool scarves his wife had knit, eggs and butter to Detroit to swap for Indian trading goods. When he returned with both his packs loaded, Mr. Ariome bubbled over with happy talk. He announced proudly, "Baptiste Ariome, he very fine trader."

He spread everything out for his wife and children to examine. Then he spun around to Jim and said, "You go with me? It is my desire have you go. I make journey among Shawnee people. Not village where you were but people of same tribe. You come speak Shawnee for me. Baptiste sell his goods for big price. You come, yes?"

What could the boy say but yes? He really had no choice, and maybe in the Indian towns he would meet a trader from the south who could give him news of his family.

When they reached the first Shawnee village, it all seemed familiar to Jim. But now he was an outsider and the red men were suspicious of him. He found he could not get enthusiastic over selling glass beads, trinkets and ribbons to the Indians. He felt sad and discouraged. All he wanted to do was to get back to Abb's Valley.

On their return to the Ariome home, the trader's wife took Jim aside and asked what was wrong. She consoled him, "Never give up your hope, Jim, to go home. I tell my Baptiste it is not wrong you have this wish. A good son must have this desire to return home. You are brave *garçon*. Do not despair."

Jim always remembered that when they were trading among the Indians. He kept his eye alert to discover anyone who could assist him in his plan to return to Virginia.

After each return to the Ariome farm in Canada, Jim felt more restless than before. As the months passed, he even had trouble sleeping at night. He dreamed of his mother and two sisters, Mary and Jane. He thought he was meeting them traveling northward and they looked as if they'd seen much trouble. This nightly dream was so real that it haunted the boy by day.

Late in the summer of 1786, Mr. Ariome took Jim on a selling trip among the Shawnees. In one village, Jim heard someone shout "Shemanese" at him. It was Big Rib, the friend of Young Wolf, the brave with whom he had hunted.

Jim asked all about Little Otter, Wapeuttequah, Young Wolf and his other friends. Big Rib answered every question and told much news of the village. But he kept his head low and did not look Jim in the eye.

"You are keeping something from me. Who is dead? What is wrong?"

At last Big Rib faced Jim and said very solemnly, "Your father killed. Some children too. Your home burned. Braves brought your mother and sisters north, made them captives like you."

So that was why he had been feeling so desperately miserable. No wonder he had dreamed of his mother and sisters heading northward.

Jim was like ice. He stared at Big Rib and demanded, "Black Wolf?"

"Black Wolf chief of raiding party. He know way to your valley. Bring other young woman too."

Jim tried to think fast who this could be. He remembered the daughter of a far neighbor who sometimes helped his mother.

He asked fiercely, "Was young woman Martha Evans?"

The Indian did not respond. Jim kept on trying to find out. He repeated the name "Martha" over and over for Big Rib to catch the sound.

Finally the Shawnee nodded, "Mar-tha, yes, that name they call girl."

Jim knew he had kept on talking about Martha Evans just to try to keep from facing the horror about his father. He asked, "My mother, my two sisters and girl Martha now in Shawnee villages, yes?"

Big Rib hung his head again. Finally he said, "Now two there. Cherokees come camp near our village. They been on hunt, find no meat. They very angry with white men. They see captives in our village. They make big threat, pull trick. Cherokees seize your mother and one sister and burn at stake. Then Cherokees leave quick."

It was too awful to believe—burned at the stake. Oh, no, not that. The boy closed his eyes as he felt everything sway around him. Gritting his teeth, he managed to pull himself together. He clutched at Big Rib and brokenly asked, "My sister Mary alive? They no kill?"

The Indian grinned in relief and said, "Little Maree my friend."

Jim Moore felt sick. His home and family almost wiped out. He tried to force himself to think of Mary. Well, at least *she* was alive, his favorite of all the family. He had even given her a pet nickname, Polly.

"You tell Mary she and I be together soon," Jim said to Big Rib as they parted.

It took the boy weeks to get over the shock of the horrible news. He was in a complete daze. He dragged around doing the chores at the farm. Gradually his mind began to function clearly again. He tried to persuade Mr. Ariome to make a trip to the village where Big Rib had said Mary was being kept.

Mr. Ariome was not willing. He protested, "Much too dangerous. Me take you away from them once. Me come again try to get girl, maybe they kill all of us. *Mais*, Baptiste Ariome, he think it over, he sorry for little girl."

But then Mr. Ariome caught a very severe cold and it developed into pneumonia. At times he was delirious with fever. The first snow of winter fell before he began to recover. Jim knew now that Ariome would not attempt the long trip to try to buy little Mary from the Shawnee.

Each morning as he got up and looked over the

snow-covered ground, Jim vowed to rescue Mary before angry Cherokees swept in and killed her. But
how? The question beat on his brain like a blacksmith's
hammer on the anvil.

II. A Thrilling Development

One gray December afternoon, Mr. Ariome, who
dreaded catching cold again, sent Jim through the
snow to sell eggs to the keeper of a small nearby inn.
The owner said, "Boy, ye had best dry yeself out afore
ye start back through the drifts."

Jim got as near the fire as a group of men gathered
around it would permit. To his amazement he heard
one of them recounting how a Mr. Stogwell had bought
a girl from some Indians.

"Shawnees they were. Seems as how some of them
done come over into Canada. They is camped down to

the peninsula between Detroit and Lake Erie. I passed the place. The savages looked half starved. Seems that these Shawnee was burned out of their villages when a band of armed settlers, led by Logan from Kentucky, came to punish them for their thieving and murdering."

A fat man asked, "What did Stogwell give for the girl? A wretched sum, I'll wager."

Jim was bursting with questions but thought he'd better listen first and learn all he could. Now the newsbringer was speaking again. "You're dead right. The Indians was drinking and wanted more fire water. I heard they sold her for a few gallons of rum."

The fat man scratched his muddy-colored hair, "Is that Stogwell the American that moved to Canada because he spied for the British during the war?"

"The same, but the British don't hold him in high esteem neither. He must have bought the girl to work her to death."

Jim Moore could stand it no longer. He broke into the conversation and spoke.

"I ask your pardon, gentlemen, but I couldn't help hearing you talking about a Mr. Stogwell buying a captive girl from the Shawnees. They are holding a young sister of mine. Please tell me the name of the girl he bought."

The man who said he had passed the camp rubbed the stubble on his chin and replied, "Can't rightly say. Don't recall hearing it."

Jim persisted, "Would her name be Mary Moore, by any chance?"

The man looked fuddled. He muttered, "Seems like that sounds familiar but I just plain don't know."

The innkeeper, who had been eager to get in on the talk, announced, "I heard a traveler from down near Stogwell's say the girl went by the name of Mary Moore."

Jim grasped the man's arm. "Oh, that's my little sister. She's not yet ten years old."

The innkeeper looked at him in a doubting way. "Now, now lad, don't be too sure. It might not be her."

Jim tried to be patient. He said, "I feel certain it is."

The paunchy innkeeper shook his head.

"Well, if it be, a rough time I'm thinking she'll have with Stogwell. If ever he should come over this far and stop here, I'll let you know so you can come and talk to him about your sister."

Jim Moore raced back to the Ariomes'. He paid no attention to the drifts of snow that confronted him but tore through them in his eagerness to tell the news.

He burst into the Ariome home and yelled, "Clarisse, my little sister's still alive. Just think, that means I still have some family."

The French girl came running to him. Her face was nearly as excited as his. "Ah, Jim, that is *magnifique*, how you say—marvelous."

"But that isn't all. Mary belongs to a white man now instead of the Indians and she's living less than seventy miles from here. Whoops, Jemima hoecakes, is that fine!"

In his exhuberant happiness, Jim grabbed Clarisse by the waist and danced her around in a jig.

Mrs. Ariome broke in with the question, "But what Englishman is this you speak of that has made the purchase of her?"

Jim stopped the jig immediately. His face took on a serious expression. "He isn't English. He's an American who was a spy during the Revolution. He moved over here because the Americans didn't like him. At least that's what I heard at the inn. But worse than that right now is that the men all agreed he would be cruel to little Mary. I don't know which is worse the Shawnees having her or this man Stogwell."

Mrs. Ariome cast her eyes up to heaven. "Ah, *mais non*. This I must talk about with Monsieur Ariome when he comes back from the cow shed."

Clarisse, Pierre and Jim all tried to get Mr. Ariome to do something right away about Mary Moore. The trader, who was still weak from his recent pneumonia, said, "This is a great sadness, Jim, but what is it possible to do? This villain Stogwell bought your sister. That is not against the law. Did I not secure you the same way? You say he lives somewhere near seventy miles away. This is Canada and the snow is deep. It is too far to go. Maybe I would make the trip if I were well, but now I cannot. I regret. It is necessary to wait."

Clarisse, however, was more sympathetic. "As Maman often say, it is possible something good happen. Did not Mr. Belcher, the keeper of the inn, say he send for you if Stogwell come there? Maybe he knows something about Stogwell coming. Maybe he have business with this Stogwell. Courage, mon brave."

And the girl's hope came true. About three weeks

after Jim first heard the news he was working on some harness in the Ariomes' kitchen when he heard a pounding on the front door. He ran to open it.

"Heh, laddie, be you Jim Moore?" the stranger asked.

"Yes, sir, I am."

"I'm on me way home from the inn and stopped by with a message. Mr. Belcher said to tell you fellow of the name Stogwell is there bargaining for some property. Guess that's how come he's in these parts."

Jim could hardly believe his ears. "Mr. Stogwell's at the inn now?"

"What ails you, son, are you deaf? That's what I said and plainly too."

Jim Moore hurled on a heavy coat and started immediately for the inn. The minute he saw Stogwell, he felt the hair rise on the back of his neck. The man had one eye that drooped and a hard, cruel look about his thinly compressed lips. In a sharp, doubting voice he kept asking Jim, "How do I know you're really brother to the girl I've bought?"

Jim struggled to hold his temper. He described his sister exactly and ended up, "No matter how much she's in the sun, she don't freckle. And her eyes are big for a little girl."

Stogwell made no response, so Jim related to the man every detail of the girl's capture by the Shawnees just as Big Rib had told it to him. Then he told briefly about his own capture and how he had lived among the same Shawnees.

Finally Mr. Stogwell grudgingly admitted, "I reckon you're the brother she's so anxious to see. Likes to

pester me to death about it but I remind her she ain't
a free critter to go traipsing around hunting lost kin
people."

Jim felt like hitting the man. He could just imagine
how nasty he was to poor little Mary. He barely managed to hang on to himself.

"Will you permit me to see her if I can make the
trip over there? Mr. Ariome's good to me and I think
he'll let me go. Don't know exactly when, but I'll come
soon as I can."

Mr. Stogwell was suddenly very oily. "No need to
make the trip, boy. It's nigh on seventy miles and
mostly through wilderness. Besides there'd be no place
for you to stay once you got there."

Jim was not to be put off so easily. "I think I could
make it. Been on long hunts with the Indians in the
snow."

"Mebbe, mebbe, but you weren't alone. 'Taint safe.
Me, I waited long time to hitch up with a party heading thisaway. Had to come on account of business. I'll
let you in on a secret." The man leaned over in a con-
fidential way before continuing, "I'm moving next
spring to a house not far from your owner's. So, wait
peaceful-like and you'll see that sister of your'n then."

Once during the winter months Jim heard of hunters heading in the direction where Stogwell lived. The
boy tried to persuade Mr. Ariome to let him go along,
but the Frenchman stormed at him, "You no Indian
any more. You go in snow and get sick in chest like me
and maybe die like my other son. *Non, non, non.* You
cannot go."

So that ended that. He had to obey the man who

owned him. The Ariomes had been kind to him and Jim had no intention of repaying them by stealing away.

At last the snow started to melt. Each afternoon, when he had completed his work, Jim went to Mr. Belcher's inn to ask if the Stogwells had moved to the neighborhood.

One April day Mr. Belcher peered down his nose at him and said, "They moved in to the old Speers house last night. Didn't bring much furniture but they had the girl."

Jim had long before found out which property Stogwell had bought. Now he headed straight for the shabby house. His chest was heaving with excitement as he tore through the fields. When he came in sight of the house, he stopped for a second to ease his breathing. He murmured half aloud, "My little sister is in there—the only member of my family the Indians left alive."

When Jim knocked, a dirty-looking woman opened the door a narrow crack. Jim quickly explained his mission. Mrs. Stogwell declared suspiciously, "My husband ain't home and I don't never let nobody in 'lessen he be here."

The boy put his foot against the open door and announced boldly, "Your husband promised I could see my sister as soon as you got here and I insist on it."

That was evidently the tone of authority the woman understood, for she grudgingly opened the door. Just behind her stood a little girl. The boy could not believe his eyes. This emaciated child in a ragged dress was his sister.

Jim was so shocked by Mary's appearance that he could not speak, and the child stared at him as if she were beholding a vision. Her large eyes searched him to make sure he was the boy she had not seen for nearly three years.

Jim said in the tenderest way, "Mary, my little sister."

He did not use his old nickname of Polly to her. It seemed too jolly for this pitiful-looking child.

The sound of his voice made her sure of him. She flew to him and flung her arms around him. He leaned over and petted her. She smothered his face with pitiful, hungry little kisses.

"Let's go out in the yard, Mary. I'll lend you my jacket. We can be by ourselves there."

Jim poured out questions. He knew he could not get the whole story at one time, but chiefly he wanted now to hear how the Stogwells were treating her.

"Sometimes, Jim, I'm so hungry I strain the water in which I wash the dishes for scraps of bread or grease to eat."

The boy had to turn his head away to hide tears in his eyes.

"Oh, brother, it was awful when they carried you away. Papa tried to get together a party of men to come after you, but there was a rumor that there was another band of Indians on the prowl that might raid on the Bluestone. The men from there couldn't leave and they warned Papa not to try. He and Simpson did search for four days but they never could find a trace. I cried every night for weeks."

"Well, here I am, safe and sound and seventeen

years old. The Ariomes, who own me, feed me good victuals. Maybe I can save mine for you."

Mary instantly responded in the same sweet little voice she had always had, "Jim, it pleasures me greatly that you're strong and healthy. And our brother Joe will be well fed at Grandma and Grandpa's."

Jim almost jumped out of his skin. He asked excitedly, "What are you saying about Joe? Wasn't he killed by the Shawnees when they shot Pa and Mr. Simpson?"

"No. 'Twas God's own mercy and nothing else. Joe had begged Papa to take him when he drove the horses back to Rockbridge to sell in the spring. Grandma asked Papa to leave him with her until he came again. So Joe was not in Abb's Valley on that horrible June day."

"I must have misunderstood what Big Rib told me. Oh, Mary, that means there are three of us Moores left. Some day we're going to be together again."

"Oh, yes, indeedy," Mary replied in such a strange way that Jim knew she didn't believe it.

That night when he finished telling Mrs. Ariome about Mary, he stood with clenched fists and yelled, "I hate that man. He's worst than any beast. That poor little starved girl, she was better off with the Indians."

From then on Jim visited his sister as often as he could. Sometimes Mrs. Stogwell wouldn't let the child come out in the yard, and she never permitted her to stay more than a few minutes. But on each visit, Jim took food which Mrs. Ariome had given him. The Ariomes were poor but they did have enough to eat. The boy slipped these bits of food to Mary on the sly so that Mrs. Stogwell would not rush out and take them for herself.

Gradually Jim tried to find out everything that had happened to his family.

One day when Mary had told him a good deal he pressed her further. "Big Rib told me that Black Wolf had also captured Martha Evans at our house. How did that happen?"

"Well, Papa had ridden over on the Bluestone and fetched Martha to help Mother sew the cotton clothes for summer. You should have seen Martha the day of the raid. She yanked up the trap door to the pit under the floor of the cabin and pulled me down in there. But I had the baby in my arms and the baby kept whimpering. Martha pushed the door up again and someway crawled out of the cabin. She hid behind that rock ledge not far from the spring. She thought an Indian had discovered her and gave herself up. On the trail, Jim, she was such a comfort to me when they tomahawked and scalped little John, who was too sickly to keep up. It nearly killed me to see that Shawnee carrying his scalp swinging from his belt. And poor baby Margaret kept crying so they dashed her brains out."

The little girl broke down in sobs at the horrible memory. Jim quickly went on to another subject. He knew that the child must not dwell on these brutalities that she had witnessed.

He asked, "Is Martha still with the Shawnees in their new camp?"

"Oh, no. They sold her before they did me. A dreadful man named Caldwell bought Martha from the Indians. But the other day Mr. Stogwell was tormenting me by claiming that some English people near here have bought Martha from Caldwell. He kept telling me how rich they were. He might have made up the whole tale because he doesn't often tell the truth."

"Yes, but maybe for once he has told the truth. There is a family of wealthy English named Donaldson living not far away. I'll go there and see."

"Oh, please do. Martha is the best friend I could ever have."

Mr. Ariome went with Jim to the home of the well-do-do Donaldson family. Yes, it was true that they had bought Martha Evans from Caldwell.

"We heard how cruel he was and we needed someone to serve in our household. We have given Martha her freedom and pay her wages for working for us."

That very day Jim was able to take Martha to see young Mary. Martha, who was about nineteen, was just as furious as Jim over the way the Stogwells treated the small girl, especially at the whippings they gave her.

Months passed and the situation did not improve. One day, to his surprise, Jim found an ally in a man who had been in the Stogwell home and seen the way they were treating Mary. This man was Simon Girty. At first Jim did not even wish to speak to the man, for he had often heard his father call Simon Girty a traitor for his actions during the Revolution. The man's name was notorious up and down the frontier. But for some reason Girty's hard heart had been touched by little Mary, or maybe he wanted to get even with Stogwell on some old score.

Jim had been sent to the inn to sell eggs. Simon Girty

called him over to his table saying, "I know your story, boy. I strongly advise ye to make a full complaint against Stogwell for the way he's misusing your little sister. If you don't, 'tis not likely she'll last long in this world."

"But, Mr. Girty, where could I make such a complaint?"

"To Colonel McKee, the British agent for Indian affairs. She was sold by the varmints across the border into Canada, so McKee's your man."

The boy got new hope from this advice of something to do. He hoped that he could persuade Colonel Mc-Kee to set his sister free. It took some time before he could get permission to present the complaint to the official. Simon Girty accompanied the boy.

Finally the powerful British officer set trial for Stogwell, who was severely reprimanded for his cruelty. Word leaked out that after the trial the colonel said, "You're within the law, Stogwell, to own the child, but His Majesty's government does not tolerate cruelty. What is more, if any chance should ever come for this scrap of a girl to be taken back to her own people in Virginia, I hereby order that you are to release the child without ransom. I wish to hear of no bargaining going on. Is the order understood?"

After that Stogwell knew he was being watched and had to act more humanely toward little Mary. Jim was afraid that the man might try to stop him seeing his sister. But he did not. Ariome said he thought this was because Stogwell was trying to get back in favor with McKee and ask for a job.

Jim hated to see the summer of 1787 wane because

he dreaded the winter for Mary. When the severe cold set in, he and Martha could visit the girl very little.

For him it was different. The winter evenings with the Ariomes, with Clarisse singing and teasing him, were so pleasant that Jim wondered why he should struggle to go back to Virginia. His home was burned and nearly all his family wiped out. He began to wonder if Clarisse thought of him just as a replacement for her brother, or was she fond of him in a different way?

But then he would go again to see Mary and the sight of her misery would make him realize that he must do all possible to get the girl away. He hoped that maybe the following summer they could leave.

It was a late August day and Jim felt full after a big midday meal. Clarisse had fixed his favorite dishes. He would sit on the front steps and whittle a while before he went back to the fields to work. He wanted to think, for the summer was nearly gone and Mary was still with the Stogwells. But Colonel McKee and the court had ruled that Mary could be freed only if there was a way for her to go to Virginia.

The eighteen-year-old boy groaned. How could he take her without horses, how could he buy horses without money, and how could he himself, owned just as she was, secure money?

Jim glanced around the yard. Though it was still warm while the sun was out, the leaves of the trees and bushes showed signs that the summer of 1788 was nearly over. If he was going to try to do anything, he'd have to act quickly or wait till spring.

The only way he could possibly do it would be to borrow the money. Would Mr. Ariome lend him that much? No, the Ariomes didn't have that much money to spare. They were struggling to pay for the farm.

Did he dare approach Mr. Donaldson for the loan of money? The wealthy man would have no reason to believe that Jim could secure funds in Virginia or get the money back up here to him. And how could he, one boy, protect the girls on the long trip if they should encounter wild animals or run into Indians?

Jim flung his knife into the ground in disgust. There was just no way to do it. The realization of his hopelessness was bitter to the boy.

He leaned to pick up his knife and heard a clip-clop sound. Then he heard happy voices talking. Who in the world would be riding up at this time of the day?

In a moment he was to have the answer. He saw Martha Evans jump down from a horse she had been riding, behind a young man. She ran across the yard toward him.

"Jim, Jim, my brother has come all the way from Virginia for me." The girl's face was radiant with joy and her words tumbled out in a cascade.

The boy was thunderstruck. He muttered stupidly, "Your brother—that big tall fellow in the deerskin clothes?"

"Yes, Thomas Evans. Oh, Jim, here's our chance at last. He's come to rescue us, all the way from the Blue-stone and home."

At last Jim believed her. He bounded out to the

horseman, who was tying his reins around a fence post. The boy offered his hand to the fine-looking frontiersman.

"How in thunderation did you ever find where Martha was, much less get all the way up here from Virginia?"

It took all afternoon for Thomas Evans to tell his story, egged on by one question after another from his sister or Jim. Mrs. Ariome declared that it was a holiday for everyone, and all the Ariomes gathered to listen to the bronzed man tell of his search. Clarisse served cold milk and some tarts she had made.

Thomas Evans gave a full account of the horror felt up and down the frontier over the Shawnee massacre of Captain Moore and the carrying off of the family. He related the vain efforts they had made to overtake the raiding party.

"All that summer, 1786, I kept trying to figure out how to come after you, Martha. You recall that Ann Crow and I had pledged ourselves and were figuring on getting married soon's we could. But Ann calculated I would never be happy 'less I tried to find you. She's the finest girl anyone ever had. She kept right on encouraging me to start out even though we both had our hearts set on getting married. So she helped me get everything ready and that September I took out.

"Everybody was interested in the trip, of course. The men decided I'd better not take a rifle because the Indians would more likely believe I was on a peaceful mission if I didn't."

"You started out into the wilderness with no rifle?" Jim asked incredulously.

"That's right, but I had a knife and tomahawk in my belt, a knapsack on my back and a pistol hidden under my leather shirt."

"How'd you know where to head?" Jim asked.

"Wasn't certain at all. But we were sure the Shawnees had taken you up toward the Ohio so I headed that way."

Thomas told how he had fallen in with Simon Girty and a man named Conoly and traveled all that fall and winter with these men. They had visited twenty Shawnee villages but could find no trace of his sister.

Clarisse handed him a glass of milk and the tall frontiersman continued.

"Well, I saw I wasn't getting nowhere. In the late spring I heard there was going to be a meeting of Indians and white men on the border of Kentucky. The meeting was for the settlers to ransom captives that the red varmints were holding."

Jim shook his head. "I didn't know they did that."

Martha said excitedly, "Go on, Thomas, what happened there?"

"Sister, I really danced a jig at that meeting when I ran smack dab into a fellow who'd been a prisoner of the Shawnees. He told me you'd been sold to a white man in Canada up here near Detroit. He ain't never even heard of you, Jim, but he thought little Mary was up this way too."

Martha's eyes were gleaming. "And did you start up here right then?"

"That I did not. I was on foot. I knew it would take a horse and money to get as far as Canada. So I headed back to Virginia. It took me all that summer and the next winter to get together what I needed for the long trip here. But last spring, April, 1788, to be exact, I started off again. I was riding the best horse we owned."

Mrs. Ariome broke in to announce, "Jim, I regret, but it is time for Clarisse to milk the cows, and Pierre, you must hurry and bring me wood for the cooking of supper."

Martha clapped her hand to her mouth. "Oh, brother, I must go back to prepare food for the Donaldsons. I've been gone a long time."

Thomas Evans strode up to the shabby Stogwell house and announced to the droopy-eyed man who opened the door that he wished to see Mary Moore. Evans immediately made it clear why he had come from Virginia; and Stogwell, remembering Colonel McKee's order, let him see the small girl. Thomas and Mary joined Jim and Martha, who were waiting in the yard, and together they talked over all the possibilities of getting back to Virginia.

Leaving the Stogwell place after the talk, Thomas Evans turned to Jim. "I've only got the one horse. If I buy another for my sister, can you purchase one for you and Mary? She's so little she could ride behind you or maybe the two girls could ride the same mount."

"Thomas, I hate to tell you but I haven't a shilling. Mr. Ariome feeds and clothes me, but that's all."

This was serious. Without another horse the trip would not be possible, but the two young men went steadily on with their planning. Thomas went first to see Colonel McKee to make sure that Stogwell would have to free Mary Moore without ransom. Then he checked with Mr. Donaldson about Martha. The prosperous Englishman assured Thomas that he did not wish and would not accept money for releasing Martha. And, from the beginning, the Ariomes had promised Jim that he would not have to buy his freedom.

So now Thomas announced to the young captives, "It appears like I'll have just enough money to buy a horse for you, Jim, as well as the one Mr. Ariome's found for the girls."

Mrs. Ariome was all smiles. She kept saying, "Jim, I told you not to despair. Now you will be going home and taking poor *petite* Mary."

Each time she said that, Jim felt deceitful. For nearly four and a half years he had dreamed of going back to Virginia. Now he didn't want to leave Clarisse. She was so pretty and so gay. He thought maybe she liked him in a special way too. But he knew that Mary must be taken home, and now the problem was to provide warm clothing to protect her on the long trip. Mrs. Donaldson heard about it and gave him a thick woolen cape her daughter Betsy had outgrown. Clarisse cut down a warm dress of her own to fit the small eleven-year-old girl.

But their start was held up by their search for another horse at the price Thomas Evans could afford to pay. Finally Mr. Donaldson let them buy one of his.

It was none too soon. Mr. Belcher, the innkeeper, had overheard a whispered conversation. He warned Thomas about it.

"Them rogues I heard talking said the son of Simon Girty had employed Indians to ambush the four of ye on the trail. They are only to get their money if they kills the two of ye young men and brings the girls back to be sold again."

The delay was unbearable. Then one morning Thomas came downstairs at the inn, where he'd been staying, to find Mr. Belcher plying a man with drink. The innkeeper held up his finger to his lips. "Sh-h-h, I'm trying to dig news out of him about the Girtys. He knows something valuable."

Finally the man was drunk enough to tell what he knew. Three days ago Simon Girty and his son had quarreled terribly. Some said it was about money, some said it was because the boy thought he had outsmarted his old man and had schemed a plot that Simon didn't like. Anyhow, Simon had denounced his son, and the next day young Girty had been found hanging from a tree, dead by suicide.

That was all Thomas Evans needed to hear. He rushed out of the tavern to tell the others to get ready to leave. The Girty son could no longer carry out his plot against them.

12. Goal Achieved

The air was crisp with chill the mid-October day they left. Jim Moore was the only one who was not in high spirits. He wrestled with the idea of asking Clarisse to wait for him. But he knew he might never even reach Virginia, much less get back to Canada.

And so he just kept his eyes glued on the French girl as if he could not have enough of looking at her. She was puzzled over his behavior, but she still tried to smile and be gay. Finally he blurted out to her, "You know what I feel. Oh, it's so dreadful to leave you. I want to come back. You know that, don't you?"

The girl pulled his head down to kiss him. He took

her in his arms and kissed her in a way that left no
doubt about how he felt.

Thomas was shouting, "Jim, Jim, where are you?
We must leave at once."

And there was no time to lose, for Thomas had arranged for Jim and Mary to travel for the first lap of
the trip with a company of traders going by boat to the
Moravian towns on the opposite side of Lake Erie.

As they rode toward the point where the boat was
waiting, Jim explained, "They call the Indians in those
villages the Moravians because they've been converted
to Christianity by the Moravian missionaries. They'll
be friendly to us. Mary and I will wait for you there.
We'll take the saddlebags so you can ride fast."

The four were reunited, as planned, at a Moravian
Indian village in the region of Sandusky.

Little Mary became a favorite among the Moravian
Indians. She showed them the battered small New
Testament which she had rescued from her burning
home in Abb's Valley and brought with her.

Thomas Evans could not stop marveling over the
fact that the girl had managed to keep it. "I would
have thought the Injuns would've snitched it from
you," he often said.

"They tried to," Mary told him, "but there was an
old chief who used to ask me to 'Make the book talk,'
and each time he made the snatchers give it back to
me."

Martha Evans told Thomas and Jim, "It's my belief
that that book kept Mary from losing her reason after
the horrors she saw."

Even the chief of the village liked to talk to the

child, explaining how the Moravian Indians wanted to live at peace with the white men and their red brothers too.

While Mary talked with the chief, Jim became acquainted with the hunters of the village. He learned that a party of them were about to start on their fall hunt and for a part of the way would follow a route much the same as their own. But the Indian hunting party would not be ready to start for several days.

Jim told the Evanses, "Indians who hate white men often hunt and camp in the section we've got to go through."

Little Mary said solemnly, "Simon Girty's son killed himself but those Indians he hired might still show up and kill you boys and carry Martha and me back to captivity. The Moravian Indians will protect us if we're with them. The chief told me they would."

All admitted that ambush was a possibility, and they waited to travel with the hunting party.

At last they were on their way again. Jim was back in his element. He knew the woods and what to watch for. He was the first to see signs that another hunting party of Indians had passed that way. That night, they camped near the other hunters. This did not worry the peaceful Moravians, but it did bother Jim and Thomas Evans. They decided to keep watch and divided the guard duty between them.

Jim had the early morning shift and, in the half light that precedes the dawn, saw five warriors leave the other camp and start through the woods. He gave instant warning to the Moravians, who went forward to meet the visitors.

The girls hid in a thicket of elders and Thomas guarded them while Jim walked boldly across the clearing and listened in on the conference between the painted braves and the gentle Moravians. The warriors demanded possession of the white people. The Moravian Indians absolutely refused to give up their friends. The painted men repeated their demands in various ways and even offered a bribe. But nothing changed the determination of the Moravians, and the smaller warrior deputation finally went away, uttering threats as they stalked off.

After that, the Moravian Indians moved more rapidly. When the point was reached where the Virginians had to turn off to head for Fort Pitt, they hated to separate from the friendly red men. All four young people thanked their escorts but little Mary pleased the hunters the most when she said, "Good-by, my good Christian friends."

Jim and Thomas figured that they now had five solid days of travel before reaching the first settlements in Pennsylvania. This was wilderness country and they all knew that the danger of warlike Indians, snakes and wild beasts was very present. So they proceeded on the alert.

On the third day, Jim was riding at the head of the party when he wheeled in the saddle to signal "Indians ahead." He pointed to a place where a party of redskins had recently camped. They rode up to the remains of the fire.

Thomas said, "The coals are still hot."

Jim shook his head. "This is bad; they left here barely two hours ago. It's just about eleven now. They may know of our coming and be up ahead lying in wait by the side of the trail. They must be the ones that threatened the Moravians for us."

Thomas pulled out the crude copy of Colonel Mc-Kee's map that they had made before leaving Canada. They carefully studied the streams that would guide them in case they were separated from each other. The two boys worked out a plan of action if they were attacked by day, another plan if the Indians swooped down on them by night.

All day they proceeded with even greater care than before and stopped early so they could put out their cook fire before darkness fell. The girls wrapped themselves in their blankets and stretched out on the cold ground. The boys sat with blankets around them and their guns across their knees. None of the party had fallen asleep when they heard footsteps coming down the trail and Martha whispered, "Sounds like a man walking extra careful."

Her brother nodded in agreement and cocked his rifle.

Nearer and nearer the footsteps came. Jim could see that Mary was praying. It wrung his heart. The poor little girl had been through so much. The boy wondered whether all their efforts to get home would end here in this spot in the forest.

Suddenly the approaching figure stopped. There was no movement or sound of any kind. Silence hung like an evil cloud.

Jim laid his hand on Thomas' shoulder in their signal for action and the two young men rose to charge the enemy. The silence was shattered by a snort and the crashing noise of an animal bounding away in the brush.

Jim shouted, "A deer, probably a big buck. Not even an Indian can imitate that snort."

Thomas made a tiny fire and used some dead leaves as a torch. By that light they easily found the trail of the buck. The relief over its not being an Indian was almost too much. The four sank down by the fire. Martha sobbed convulsively for a few minutes but Mary comforted her. The boys acted as if they didn't hear, for they knew that it was better to leave the girls alone for a while.

The next day was peaceful. They found no more trace of the traveling Indians on the trail and decided the other party must have veered off to the west. That night, by their small campfire, the four young people felt safe enough to relax. Martha started humming a little tune she had learned in Canada.

The sound upset Jim. It was one of the tunes that Clarisse had sung to him. All down the trail he had pushed away the memory of her as often as he could. Thomas fortunately began talking and Martha stopped humming the song.

"Well, by tomorrow night, we should be within the frontier settlements of Pennsylvania."

Martha said joyfully, "Oh, imagine spending the night in a real American home again."

Little Mary burst in impulsively, "Oh, Thomas, I can never thank you enough for hunting so hard for us. I'll never forget it."

Thomas Evans was a tease, and now that he felt the worst danger was over he jokingly replied, "Ah, Mary,

when you get back to Virginia you'll be with your
grandparents and uncles and aunts with their fine farms
and horses and you'll soon forget me."

He turned around and by the firelight noticed that
the little girl was crying, but she managed to say, "No,
Thomas, whatever may happen to me I will never forget you. If I ever have a home of my own, the door will
always be open to you."

Jim Moore laid his big hand on his sister's shoulder.
She was a solemn little girl from all the terror she had
witnessed.

The four proceeded on the next day to the settlements near Fort Pitt and soon reached the home of
an uncle and aunt of Thomas and Martha Evans.
The relatives made a huge fuss over Martha, who had
been through so much, and over Thomas for having
accomplished the rescue. They tried to be nice to Jim
and Mary too, but Jim suspected that the aunt was
resentful toward the Moore family for having been the
cause of Martha's capture.

Mary was concerned because she and Jim were
crowding the Evanses, whose frontier home was very
small. But Thomas said they could not leave until the
horses were rested. Neighbors came from all around to
see and talk to these young Virginians who had lived
through such amazing experiences.

Jim found it good to be back among people who
spoke much like the people back home. Yet always he
missed Clarisse.

The plan had been for the four to stay with the
Evanses only a short while, but bad luck caught up
with them while they were there. First one of their

horses injured his foot on a sharp stick and they had to wait for the wound to heal. Just about the time the horse was ready for use, Thomas Evans dislocated a shoulder while felling a tree.

The frontiersman was furious with himself. He growled, "How could I have done such a thing? Me who has felled as many trees as a beaver."

The shoulder was so badly out of place that it gave great pain, and Thomas could not hide his misery.

"Back home on the Bluestone I know a feller could snap this thing right back where it ought to be and he's not a doctor either."

But when they found a local man who said he knew how to pull the shoulder back, he went about it too fiercely to suit Jim Moore. The great burly farmer made one tug and got nowhere. Thomas Evans' face was white from the pain.

The huge man tried again. Jim was standing by Thomas to catch him if he should fall from the pain. As the man made his second great yank, Jim distinctly heard a sharp snap.

Thomas let out a low sickening moan and gasped, "My arm—it's broken, broken right here above the elbow."

The would-be helper shook his head. "Sure am sorry. I've yanked many a one back and this ain't never happened before. Guess some days I can't do nothing right."

There was utter silence in the cabin, for Jim and Mary, Thomas and Martha knew only too well what this meant. Thomas' uncle beckoned to Jim and they set out down the road to borrow a wagon. Jim drove his suffering friend into Fort Pitt, where they were able to find a surgeon. The medical man shook his head. "Dad blast these rough woodsmen who try to play doctor. Clumsy work by an unskilled chap."

It was a painful business dealing with the shoulder, which was still dislocated, and the newly broken arm. Thomas sweated through the ordeal and Jim suffered almost as much watching him.

The surgeon ordered Thomas to stay close by for a few days, declaring, "No bumpy travel out to your uncle's until I say so or I wash my hands of you."

The arm was troublesome and, in addition to being painful, made Thomas awkward. It meant, of course, that he could do little for himself. After a few days, Thomas returned to his uncle's home, but the weeks dragged for him. He could only watch the other three trying to do enough work to pay for their board and keep.

After the prescribed time, Jim took Thomas back into the settlement of Fort Pitt, located where the Monongahela and Allegheny merge to form the Ohio River. The surgeon was not pleased with the degree of healing that Thomas' arm and shoulder had reached. When Thomas said he simply had to leave for Virginia, the surgeon snorted and replied, "Not unless you want permanent injury. You just aren't fit to travel down that miserable road to Winchester. Why, settlers along there are still as rare as an honest man. If you intend to be an active man in the future, there's only one course. Wait until spring."

Jim's heart plummeted. This really was the worst they could have figured on. They had come so far only to be holed up in the Evanses' small home for the winter. It was a grim prospect but Jim struggled not to let his friend see how he felt. Thomas was in a bigger hurry than he, for at the end of the trip Ann Crow would be waiting. For the thousandth time, Jim wished he could ride back to Clarisse.

That winter the boy from Abb's Valley trapped, hunted, fished through the ice and helped Mr. Evans. Paying for his and Mary's board in this way relieved him, but Jim could save no money for the rest of the trip. Due to the surgeon's fees and the cost of boarding in town, Thomas was running short on funds.

When spring finally came, Thomas made a hard decision. He had only enough money to get the Moores to Virginia. He would make a fast trip with them and then come back for his sister. The aunt and uncle urged Martha to stay and she consented. Jim had often said to Thomas, "If there's any money left in my family, I know they will give you everything they can for what you've done."

Before, Thomas had always grown irritated with Jim for saying this, declaring, "I'm no Indian. I don't want bounty for bringing you two back safely." But now Jim insisted that any sensible man would accept money for expenses, and Thomas finally agreed he would accept as much as he needed to return for Martha, so that the two of them could get back to their home on the Bluestone River.

The girls clung to each other before parting. The Moores felt badly riding off with Thomas and leaving Martha behind, but Thomas said, "I'll get back."

The three travelers rode through Mount Braddock

and down to the old Cumberland Road, which they reached near Fort Necessity. Thomas and Jim got all excited when they came to Great Meadows, the site of the fort. Thomas' grandfather had fought in the French and Indian Wars and had brought him up on tales of George Washington. It made the way shorter that they were traveling a road the great hero had taken on his way to Fort Necessity.

Finally they reached Fort Cumberland and started down the Maryland side of the Potomac. They spent that night in a farm home and in the morning had to wait for breakfast. The boys went out to water the horses and Mary sat down to read her New Testament. They made a hurried departure as soon as they had eaten. They were miles down the road before Mary cried out, "Oh, I left my Testament. We must go back, 'tis the only thing I've got left from home. Oh, please turn back."

The girl's eyes were filled with tears. Jim was anxious to go back and get it for her, but Thomas took a firm stand. "No, we must press on. There's only one house where we can put up tonight. They warned me at the fort to get through this stretch quickly."

At last they crossed over into Virginia. Mary got down and patted the soil and in her funny serious little way said, "Oh, sacred soil that has fed my people. How I've missed walking on you these three long years."

One morning Thomas figured that by that night they could reach a family who knew the story of the captives and would welcome them as guests. So, at a crossroads, Evans bought lunch and some feed for the horses, commenting, "There goes my last coin."

Jim was worried about their lack of money but Thomas replied, "Stop fretting. We'll reach that family before dusk and receive a royal welcome."

That afternoon, a snow flurry fell and then the snow turned to rain. They were soon exceedingly wet, but Thomas kept saying, "We'll soon dry out by a friendly fire."

But when they reached the home Thomas had described, the family did not seem at all interested in the long-absent Moores even though a nephew had married into the Moore family. The woman of the house looked annoyed at their tracking in so much rain and mud and only grudgingly directed them to the fire. Conversation lagged and no invitation was given to the three youthful travelers to spend the night.

Jim could see that Thomas was furious. As for himself, he could not get out of there fast enough. He said, "I think we'd best be off right away."

The woman made some feeble mention of the rain but did not urge them to stay. The three young travelers plunged out into the storm and rode off. Daylight was already fading.

Thomas Evans announced, "If we had to ride all night I wouldn't stop and risk such rudeness again. Those folks have lived safe and snug too long. We'll somehow or other keep on until we hit your family's place."

Jim asked, "Do you think we can get to my aunt's house on Middle River? She's Mrs. William

McPheeters, you know. That's where Pa's mother and father live."

Mary assured them that she could keep going. "Oh, if only I can see Grandma and Grandpa and Aunt Rachel and Uncle William. Pa took me there to visit when I was five."

The horses were terribly weary. They kept stumbling, but the riders urged them on. It was hard to follow the narrow dirt road. They halted twice at cabins to ask the way to the McPheeters home.

It was very late when they spied the light of the house they sought.

Jim's heart was pounding with excitement as he knocked on the big front door of his aunt's home. The door was opened cautiously by Mr. McPheeters. Jim said quickly, "Uncle William, I'm your nephew James Moore of Abb's Valley."

The man burst out, "God's merciful providence, can it be so?" and flung open the door.

Little Mary rushed past him straight into the arms of her Aunt Rachel, who was standing in the hall just behind Uncle William.

Jim spied his grandmother and grandfather sitting by the fire. The boy had not seen them for many years and they seemed terribly old, but he would have known them anywhere. He went straight over to the old lady and leaned over to kiss her.

Then he said, "This is Thomas Evans, a neighbor of ours from near Abb's Valley. He never gave up searching for us and we wouldn't be here but for him."

The family showered attention and thanks on Thomas, who was very embarrassed at having such a fuss made over him. Jim's Aunt Rachel hugged Thomas even before kissing her own nephew.

At this point Jim and Mary's brother came running downstairs. Joe, now nearly as tall as Jim, rushed straight to Mary and picked her up in a big loving hug.

Mrs. McPheeters immediately set about preparing a feast worthy of the occasion. Joe volunteered to stable the horses while the travelers were made to change to dry clothes.

It was a jolly meal and an exciting evening. No one wanted to go to bed, late as it was. There was too much to talk about.

In all the happy talk, Jim could not help remembering that he would never have a homecoming like this with his mother and father or his sisters and brothers whom the Indians had killed. However, he pushed that thought back in his mind, as well as a wish that Clarisse could be with him.

The next morning Jim told his aunt and uncle how much money Thomas had spent on the trip. The family united to argue Thomas down in his reluctance to take the money.

Jim slapped the tall frontiersman on the back. "Don't be a goat, Thomas. You said at Fort Pitt that you would. You've got to go right back after Martha or I'm going myself. Neither Mary nor I'll be happy till she's back in Virginia."

A few days later Thomas rode on to the home of the children's uncle who was handling their father's estate and did accept full reimbursement for all money spent.

Jim and Mary settled down to enjoy being with their relatives. But the greatest happiness came later that summer when Thomas Evans returned with his sister Martha.

Jim let out a great whoop, like a Shawnee. "Thomas, I can see by the gleam in your eye that you're on your way to the Bluestone and a certain pretty girl named Ann. It took me five years to get back to Virginia and for Mary it was three, but watch Thomas travel to his bride-to-be!"

Thomas grinned and drawled, "Yes, and I'm thinking you might be doing that some day yourself."

But Jim's people would not hear to his going right back to Canada. There was much to be done about his father's estate and the holdings in Abb's Valley.

It was there in the bluegrass valley that Jim heard the news about Clarisse Ariome. A horse trader brought the message, "A man named Ariome told me if I ever came across you to tell you him and his wife arranged a marriage for their daughter Clarisse with some French fellow. Said as how he'd promised the girl he'd get word to you that the family made her do it."

It took a long time for the memory of the sparkling French girl to fade. But one day, back in Rockbridge, Jim met a charmer and all the past was wiped out. Her name was Barbara Taylor and she had many beaus. She was as sweet as his sister Mary and as gay as Clarisse.

Jim set to work to court the lovely Barbara. He used every wile and won. On February 16, 1797, a minister pronounced the two to be man and wife. A year later Jim Moore moved his bride to Abb's Valley, and there they built their home almost on the site of the cabin the Shawnees had so ruthlessly destroyed. Jim was happy. He would fulfill the dreams of his father and raise cattle and horses in the beautiful narrow valley.

Meanwhile little Mary was growing up. Before long she, too, married happily. She became the wife of a Presbyterian minister, the Reverend Samuel Brown, and her life was a full and busy one, for they had many children. Five of her sons went into the ministry and two served as elders. The girl who had been captured by the Shawnees had seen much that it was better to forget. But she had much to pass on, and this she did.

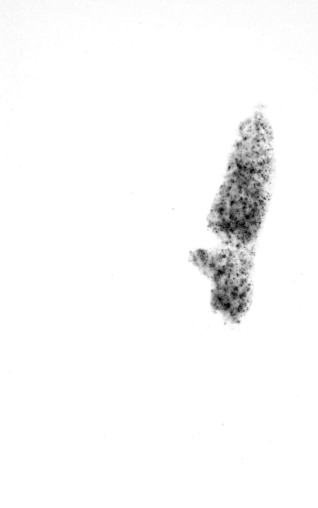